Shadows Of Betrayal

MK Maximous

Published by Mariam Khalifa, 2024.

SHADOWS OF BETRAYAL

First edition. October 17, 2024.

ISBN: 979-8227843050

Written by MK Maximous.

Table of Contents

Chapter one

Under the golden twilight sky, the luxurious villa stood as an architectural masterpiece reflecting elegance and beauty, with its gleaming white walls and wide windows overlooking enchanting landscapes. The surrounding garden was a mosaic of art, where the colors of blooming flowers intertwined with the greenery of trees and shrubs. The outdoor courtyard of the villa had been transformed into a stage for joy, with areas designated for dancing under the stars and tables covered in luxurious fabrics adorned with bouquets of flowers. In this place, family, friends, and loved ones gathered to celebrate the love story of Daniel and Violet. The atmosphere was filled with love and happiness, and the air carried the fragrance of flowers. As evening approached, the villa and its gardens were illuminated with warm, twinkling lights, adding an aura of magic and romance.

Daniel, a star shining in the realm of romance and charm, with a captivating voice that emanates from a golden throat, possessed a fair complexion that glowed like the first light of dawn. His athletic build spoke of dedication, honed by countless hours of training. His piercing blue eyes, filled with intelligence and deep emotion, drew admiration wherever they looked. When he directed his gaze towards Violet, girls' hearts melted, wishing to be in her place . His carefully trimmed black hair fell gracefully on his forehead, and his defined jawline added to his allure. Daniel shone in his elegant dark suit, which emphasized his strength and cloaked him in an aura of dignity and majesty. With his charisma and loving spirit, Daniel rewrote the rules of love, with every word and glance painting the dream picture that every lover longs for.

At the heart of this joyous gathering was Violet, the bride who appeared like the full moon in a clear sky, possessing a beauty that captivated all eyes and a charm that was hard to describe. Her dress sparkled under the lights, adorned with lace and beads that reflected the brilliance of the stars, and her tiara glittered atop her head. Her olive skin and silky, shiny black hair, each strand glistening under the moonlight as if woven with exquisite craftsmanship. Her dazzling smile revealed perfectly aligned white teeth, and her wide black eyes reflected the world's beauty, the secret to Daniel's love for her.

Arranged around the wedding canopy were breathtaking floral arrangements, blending soft colors like light pink and white with touches of green, adding a sense of elegance and sophistication. The dim, twinkling lights around the canopy resembled stars in a clear sky, embracing the backdrop and bestowing warmth and joy upon the place. Fireworks lit up the sky, decorating the night with their vibrant colors and adding indescribable joy to the celebration.

With every step they took side by side, all eyes followed them, applause filled the air, and the music danced with the beating hearts of those present, leaving behind a feeling of joy and harmony. These were not just steps but the beginning of a new journey filled with hope, love, and partnership.

Their joy was a stage where stars and celebrities shone, and their moments glowed with overwhelming happiness. Amidst this wonderful gathering, the bride and groom stood out like stars in the sky of celebration. When they reached the designated platform to complete the wedding ceremonies, and after the marriage announcement, Daniel held Violet's hand and looked at her with a gaze full of promise and loyalty, as if to assure her that all future stories would be written together, and that their love would be their refuge and strength. With simple but deeply meaningful words, they exchanged vows that would bind them for life. Ululations erupted, and voices rose with congratulations and blessings. In the distance, fireworks lit up the night sky with the colors of joy, reflecting the happiness of those unforgettable moments.

At the end of the sparkling wedding night, as the lights dimmed and the music faded into the horizon, the newlyweds headed to their new haven, their home that would witness the beginning of their journey together. Their steps were laden with dreams and the echo of the laughter that filled the night.

In the house, tranquility embraced the surroundings, and the breaths of the long night began to calm. They sat side by side, letting their thoughts flow freely as they shared a glass of drink, reflecting the gleam of hope in their eyes.

"Do you know how happy I am right now?" Daniel asked with a tone full of emotion, contemplating her sparkling eyes. Violet smiled warmly, holding his hand tenderly.

"I feel like I'm in a dream. Can it be, Daniel, that you're by my side and we'll spend our lives together?"

Daniel held her hand between his, looking at her with his tender eyes, then asked:

"What do you wish for, my love? I am here for you, and everything that is to come will be to make you happy."

Violet pondered for a moment, then said:

"I dream that this house will witness our love, the happy days, and even the challenges we will overcome together. I dream that we will be each other's support in weakness, strength, disappointment, and triumph, and that our hearts will be a warm home for each other."

She then extended her arms and gently slipped into his embrace, adding:

"And that I never leave your warm embrace."

Daniel softly kissed her forehead and said:

"I promise that everything to come will be safe and warm, and everything will be for you. Starting tomorrow, we'll travel the world together. I hope to make you the happiest person in the world, Violet."
"I am happy because I am by your side."
She then leapt from the bed with energy, her lively shout echoing in every corner of the room, announcing joyfully:
"I married Daniel, I can't believe it, am I dreaming, Daniel, or is this real?"
Daniel laughed, looking at her warmly, and said:
"I can't believe I married you, Violet, and Daniel is now at your beck and call."
On this calm evening, where the candlelight softly illuminated the room, the newlyweds were overwhelmed with a deep sense of gratitude for everything life had given them up to this moment. They looked to the future with hope and optimism, ready to face whatever the coming days might bring. Amidst this feeling of contentment, they began to prepare themselves for their morning journey.

****

With the lights dimmed and the bustle fading behind the scenes, Bella took her calm steps outside the studio. The cool evening air touched her face, lifting the weight of a long day of filming off her shoulders. After an exceptional performance and highlighting an important issue (excessive sacrifice in relationships leads to neglect and ruins relationships), she felt completely satisfied with the work she had done, yet she longed for peace and tranquility after this long day.
Bella, with her pure white skin, captured the light with a special sparkle, giving her an irresistible charm both on and off camera. With grace and confidence, she moved as if dancing like a ballerina. Her long blonde hair flowed like a cascade of liquid gold, gently embracing her face. Her slender figure reflected a balance between strength and femininity, making her stand out wherever she went. She chose her

outfits with great care, preferring pieces that elegantly highlighted her natural beauty. In every television appearance, she showed attention to detail, making her a model of refined taste and elegance, and a source of inspiration and influence for her followers.

After her tiring and exhausting day, she drove through the quiet city streets at night, reflecting on the episode she had just finished filming. Thoughts crowded her mind, but she set them aside, looking forward to the moment she would arrive at her home, her private sanctuary. Finally, she arrived at her house, where dim lights welcomed her. She left behind the world of lights and cameras to step into her warm home. She closed the door behind her, leaving the noise of the outside world behind, heading straight to the living room, where she dropped her bag comfortably beside the sofa and sighed deeply, surrendering to the feeling of safety and peace her home provided.

With tired but hopeful steps towards rest, Bella decided to head to the bedroom, where she planned to immerse herself in a warm bath to melt away the burdens of the day. On her way to the bedroom, she began to remove her hairpins one by one, letting her golden locks fall freely behind her, ready for the warm water she longed to embrace.

But, as she approached the bedroom door, she noticed it was unusually ajar. Through a small gap, a faint light and unclear sounds seeped into her senses, mixed with curiosity and rising anxiety. With each step closer to the door, her pulse quickened, signaling increasing tension.

Almost involuntarily, she extended her hand, driven by an intense desire to explore the unknown, and gently pushed the door, as if afraid it would sense her tension. Bella froze in place, her eyes widening in shock and indescribable pain. There, in the room that had witnessed her sweetest memories with her husband, she found him in the arms of another woman. Time stood still at that moment, and the silence became overwhelmingly loud with its harshness, as she tried to comprehend the cruel reality of the situation.

Her voice came out choked with anger and pain, her lips trembling, and her eyes filled with tears of betrayal, those tears that burn the heart before the cheeks, saying:
"What is this? And who is this woman? Did you bring her from the street into my home and onto my bed?"

As her husband fumbled in vain attempts to justify the unjustifiable, Bella stepped back, her heart shattered and her soul weighed down with sorrow. She recalled images of the past years, the promises, the dreams, the mutual trust, all fading like a mirage. Bella, the always elegant and radiant broadcaster, found herself now facing a situation that tested everything she believed to be stable and certain in her life. She realized then that the trust that had been the foundation of their shared life had been shattered forever.

Without looking back, and with tears streaming down her face incessantly, Bella ran out of the room, leaving behind her husband and his words, which to her sounded like delirium. The pain overwhelmed her, but she gathered the remnants of her strength to face the moment. Her steps quickened outside the house, the house that was once her refuge, now feeling suffocating. She pushed the car door open in a hurry and sped away, far from the betrayal, the pain, the memories that had turned into shards cutting her heart.

The night was dark, the roads empty. She felt dizzy, the world around her spinning as if on a different axis. Her heart pounded violently, experiencing pain that crushed her chest, and she struggled to breathe. The betrayal choked her, crushing her being. In a sudden moment, she was overwhelmed by a sense of weakness, her hands losing strength, her vision blurring. Suddenly, she lost control of the car, colliding with a massive cargo truck. The collision was violent, the windshield shattered, and she was thrown forward. Barely grasping what had happened, she lost consciousness.

Bella opened her eyes to find herself surrounded by a pale glow of white light, and the continuous echoes of medical devices reached her ears. For a moment, her mind was bewildered before she realized she was lying inside a surgery room in a hospital. Pain throbbed in her head, yet the heaviest pain was not the physical one but the deep ache of betrayal burning in her heart. She glanced around with her dim vision, trying to piece together her scattered thoughts to understand how fate had led her to this place. As the events replayed in her mind, she was once again overcome by the haze of unconsciousness.

******

On the first day the newlyweds settled into one of the most prestigious luxury hotels in Paris, their marital journey began, filled with moments of happiness and love. Upon their arrival, they were greeted by a lavish celebration organized by the hotel. This meticulously planned event was a surprise orchestrated by Daniel for Violet, in collaboration with the hotel.

They were then guided to their private suite, where the doors opened to reveal a room bathed in natural light, with a gentle breeze carrying the fragrance of flowers from the nearby gardens. The interior décor blended classical elegance with modern touches, featuring polished furniture and warm-colored fabrics that created a cozy atmosphere.

From their wide window, they enjoyed a stunning view of the city, with the majestic Eiffel Tower reaching up to the sky and the rooftops of Paris sprawling like a lively painting.

On their second day in Paris, the couple celebrated the beginning of their life together in the heart of the city. As the streets of Paris breathed under the golden sunlight, they walked hand in hand across the Pont des Arts, holding each other with determination and tenderness. The river shimmered beneath them like a mirror reflecting the sky, and the love lock they fastened to the bridge stood as a testament to their promise of eternal love. The fresh air, carrying the scent of freshly baked croissants and coffee, tempted them to stop at a small café to start their day with exchanged smiles and happiness-filled glances.

Afterwards, they strolled through Gardens, where the sunlight danced through the glossy green leaves of the trees, adding a magical dimension to their moments. They found a quiet bench by fountain, where the world around them seemed to pause, granting them privacy in the bustling city of love. They shared their laughter and dreams, each conversation bringing them closer to each other.

As evening approached, they found themselves wandering through the alleys of Montmartre, the bohemian district brimming with art and life. They stood before artists who passionately painted their canvases, each painting telling a story, each corner hiding a secret. They paused for a moment, admiring the beauty of the Sacré-Cœur Basilica as it gleamed in the twilight, embracing the city with its grandeur.

Suddenly, the serenity was broken by the ringing of Daniel's phone, causing a momentary disruption. The groom looked at the screen with anticipation, and as he raised the phone to his ear, his expression froze with shock. He heard his sister's urgent and anxious voice on the other end, saying:

"Daniel, your brother has been in an accident. Henry is in the hospital. Come quickly."

"What happened, Daniel? Why did your expression freeze like that? Who's on the phone?" Violet asked, concerned.

At that crucial moment, Daniel's calm breaths turned into gasps, as if each exhale carried a piece of pain and each inhale bore the burden of harsh reality. The shock in his eyes was not just a fleeting storm; it became a hurricane ravaging his being, sweeping away all remnants of joy that this day had held.

With heavy steps and eyes clouded with worry, Daniel ran toward the hotel, while Violet followed him with growing anxiety, calling his name with a voice filled with confusion and fear, asking him what had happened, but to no avail. He seemed like a shadow moving without a soul, each step taking him further away from the happiness they had shared moments ago.

"Daniel, wait, tell me what happened?"

Violet's trembling voice tried to penetrate the depths of Daniel's daze, in a desperate attempt to pull him back to their reality and urge him to share the reasons for his worry, but it wasn't enough to break him out of his deep reverie.

Daniel didn't stop; he didn't turn around. He continued his frantic march until they reached their room in the hotel. There, while he was hurriedly gathering their belongings, Violet's questions rained down on him. Finally, when the silence became a burden heavier than words, he turned to her with eyes drowning in a sea of despair and pain and said in a barely audible voice:

"We're returning to Egypt immediately. Henry has been in an accident."

His words struck Violet like a bolt of lightning, freezing her in place for a moment, unable to believe what she had just heard. Her heart, which had been beating with love and joy just moments before, now pounded with fear and unease. Tears began to well up at the edge of her eyes, but they didn't fall out of sorrow for Henry; they flowed heavily out of grief for the ruined honeymoon that was supposed to be their special tale and for the sudden need to cut this magical trip short. Despite this, amid the heartache and soul's groaning, she found herself helping him pack their belongings, in a silence filled with tension and deep sorrow. Many questions crawled inside her mind, crowded and jostling, but time wasn't kind enough to allow her to voice them.

In the midst of that night, which was supposed to be one of their enchanting honeymoon nights, they found themselves racing against time, heading to the airport. His heart was heavy with worry for

Henry, but his eyes carried a glimmer of hope that this crisis would end peacefully.

Daniel returned from his long journey from Cairo Airport, heading straight to the hospital his sister had mentioned. The roads he traversed felt like dark, vast tunnels, guiding him towards an unknown end. The moment he arrived at the hospital felt like a transition to an entirely different reality, a world where the echo of hurried footsteps and whispers laden with anxiety filled the corridors.

Amid the chaotic turmoil, Daniel's eyes met some familiar faces among those present in the hospital, draped in black, signaling the symbols of grief and farewell. This scene ignited a spark of sorrow and loss in his soul. Yet, a part of him resisted letting his mind accept this truth, clinging to a thin thread of hope, holding onto the idea that everything happening was just a nightmare awaiting awakening.

As his steps quickened in the corridors, his gaze collided with his sister standing at the door of the intensive care unit, her presence there, with tears streaming down her face like a cold winter cloud and her wrenching sobs, told a story that needed no explanation. Without needing words, her eyes were enough to narrate to him, through the stream of tears and trembling body, the tale of pain and loss that his heart couldn't bear.

However, her tears weren't enough to convey the depth of what she harbored inside. A powerful, piercing scream escaped from her lips, penetrating the ears of those around her, carrying all the meanings of pain and despair she was drowning in, saying:

"Henry is dead, Daniel."

"Shut up, don't say that about your brother. He's my son, not just my brother. God wouldn't break my heart this way. Where is your brother? Where?"

"In the intensive care room. They've taken off the machines and are preparing to move him to the morgue for burial."

Without any hesitation, Daniel pushed open the door to the intensive care room to find himself facing a scene that surpassed all limits of pain; his brother's lifeless body lying on the bed, surrounded by nurses preparing to move him to the morgue. A loud scream erupted from his chest, echoing through the room, as he bent over his brother's body, pleading with fate in a hoarse voice and a heart heavy with despair, begging for an unlikely mercy, for this to be just a nightmare he would wake up from.

"Get up, Henry, get up, my son, get up, my dear. Don't break my heart with your departure, don't let people say you've died. Your foolish sister is crying outside. I yelled at her and told her not to say that about you. Do you remember when you used to come to me complaining about her, saying Amelia took your toys? I used to yell at her for you. I agree, Henry, you can take my car and go out with your friends. I'll buy you your own car. Just get up, get up now."

With each word he uttered, he gently shook his brother's body, pleading for him to wake up from this eternal slumber, to return to him once more. But there was no response, only the emptiness left by his absence, which filled the room by itself. At that moment, Daniel collapsed, surrendering to the deep sorrow that enveloped him, and another nightmare was lurking; while tears streamed down his cheeks and screams permeated the air, Daniel fell beside his brother, engulfed in the agony of a sudden coma.

Chapter Two

In the cemetery, where a majestic calm enveloped the surroundings, family and friends gathered to bid farewell to young Henry in his final resting place. Beside the grave stood Amelia, Henry's sister, her hands placed over her heart heavy with grief, her lips trembling with silent prayers. Her eyes, brimming with tears, watched in anguish as her brother's coffin was lowered. Her face, etched with sorrow, told a story of loss beyond words; the loss of her brother Henry, who had been so full of life and ambition.

Meanwhile, far away within the cold walls of the hospital, Daniel lay in a coma, far removed from the pain tearing at his sister's heart. He was supposed to be there, standing by Amelia, witnessing the farewell to his younger brother, sharing in the prayers and grief. But fate had another vision; one that no one had foreseen.

As the funeral rites concluded and the final moments of farewell began, friends gathered around Amelia, embracing her in a bid to plant a sense of comfort in her heavy heart.

With the setting sun, Amelia found herself walking through the long, quiet corridors of the hospital. Each step carried a weight heavier than the last; her body screamed with exhaustion, her mind weary from the sorrow gripping her heart, and her spirit searched for a strength she didn't know she possessed. After the exhausting day of burying Henry, her thoughts tugged at her; the painful memories, the happy moments that would never return, and the harsh reality she now had to face. Amelia didn't think of going home and lying in her bed, despite the physical and emotional exhaustion that threatened to overtake her.

Instead, she found herself heading towards the hospital, dragging her feet but with a strange determination. Daniel, her older brother, who lay unconscious in a coma, seemed to need her more than ever, and she needed him too.

Reaching the room where Daniel lay, she looked through the glass before entering. The machines emitted their regular sounds, those sounds that reflected Daniel's heartbeat but revealed nothing of his dreams or thoughts trapped behind the walls of unconsciousness. She stood there, watching him with tired yet love-filled eyes, wishing for him to wake up, to come back to her. In that moment, grief and hope battled within her; she wanted to scream her pain but chose instead to whisper silent prayers for her brother.

As her eyes followed the indicators of the heart monitor, her memory wandered far, delving into the depths for a missing face, Violet, her brother's wife, whom she hadn't seen since they returned from their trip. She carried a suspicion in her heart that Violet's absence from Henry's funeral might be due to her caring for Daniel in the hospital. But reality painted a different picture. As Amelia scanned the hospital corridors, scrutinizing every face she encountered, she found no trace of Violet.

Amelia stood for a moment, contemplating this puzzling absence. Then, with a trembling hand and a heavy heart, she deliberately pulled out her phone and pressed Violet's name. The phone rang several times before an answer came, Violet's tired voice barely awake as she said:

"Yes, Amelia, have you finished your brother's burial ceremony?"

The question hit Amelia like a shock, tinged with an indifference that cut deep into her feelings and sorrows. Violet should have been there, standing by her and her husband during this ordeal, yet she responded with a calmness that belied the gravity of the situation:

"Yes, I finished the burial ceremony. Where are you, Violet?"

After returning from the exhausting trip, I went to my parents' house to rest, which is why I couldn't attend the funeral. Oh, by the way, do you know? Shortly after you left, a large number of journalists gathered in front of the hospital, all looking for any news about Daniel's condition. I don't know who leaked the information, but it spread like wildfire and became the talk of all the media outlets and social media platforms. Everyone is talking about his condition while he's in a coma. If you want to see for yourself, you can check it—I've received a lot of interview requests from different news channels. It seems I've become almost as famous as your brother. When I was beside him at the wedding, everyone was wondering who I was. But now, no one needs to ask—everyone knows me. I've become famous.

Amelia stood alone, her phone suddenly feeling like a weight in her hand. Violet's voice, once a source of security and friendship before she became her sister-in-law, now echoed in her ears, distant and unfamiliar. The words she had hoped would offer comfort and support instead transformed into a cold barrage, sending chills through her heart.

Violet's question about her brother's burial, raised as a secondary matter, was a blow Amelia wasn't prepared to receive. In an unconscious movement, without thinking, she found her finger pressing the end call button. The phone went silent, but the echo of shock and disappointment caused a noise in her chest, filling the space with a painful buzz. She couldn't bear any more, nor comprehend any other words that might come from Violet, the friend she had hoped would be her companion in grief.

Amelia found herself standing at the threshold of the intensive care room where her brother Daniel lay, her heart pounding with indescribable pain. She crept into the room with heavy steps, each step bringing her closer to Daniel, weighing her down with loneliness and despair.

The dim lights in the room and the sounds of the machines connected to Daniel that monitored the minutest details of his life filled her with fear of experiencing the pain of separation again. Amelia stood by Daniel's bedside, watching him in silence, contemplating his calm features that hid behind them a storm of events that had brought them here.

Then, without any preamble, the barriers holding back the waves of sorrow collapsed. Amelia burst into bitter tears, her tears flowing abundantly, expressing a pain that words couldn't describe. Her sobs came from the depths of a heart heavy with grief, a heart that had lost a brother and feared losing another.

Her broken whispers and the tears that wet Daniel's hands all carried a message of love and determination, a message from a sister to her brother, begging him not to give up, to come back from his distant journey to where life still pulsed with hope.

Between her sobs, Amelia began to speak to Daniel in a broken voice, as if trying to convey her message to his soul, hoping it would reach his consciousness trapped behind the walls of the coma, and saying: "Daniel, I need you so much. Don't leave me too, Daniel. I'm alone and I'm scared. I'm afraid you'll fail the test and succumb to death. Please, don't leave me."

****

In the heart of the hospital, where life and death play their eternal game, the operating room was witnessing a frantic battle to keep Bella, the well-known energetic broadcaster, alive. Inside the room, the atmosphere was filled with palpable tension as doctors and nurses moved efficiently and swiftly, each entirely focused on their role in this desperate attempt to save a life hanging by a thread.

On the operating table, Bella lay pale and still, in stark contrast to the vibrant image the public was accustomed to seeing. The surrounding machines emitted intermittent sounds, heightening the tension, while the doctors worked diligently, moving from one instrument to another, trying to restore the rhythm of life to her body.

Outside the operating room, Bella's father, mother, and sister Emma stood in the hospital corridor, powerless to do anything but wait and pray. The anxiety was evident on their faces, and with each passing minute, the pain and despair in their eyes grew. Her mother silently screamed, while her father tried to remain stoic, but his trembling lips and tear-filled eyes betrayed his inner torment. Emma, wearing her worry like a heavy coat, stood in the hospital lobby, each passing second feeling like an hour, and every sound in the corridors felt like a harbinger of news that could shake her balance. Bella, who had always been the other half of her soul, was fighting for her life in the operating room, and Emma could only wait. Her gaze shifted between the clock and the door, torn between hope and despair, afraid of losing her sister and the void her absence would leave. In those moments, Emma realized the depth of her bond with her sister, not just a blood connection, but a spiritual one that couldn't be destroyed. In those terrifying moments, they looked towards the door with hope, wishing for good news, while the doctors inside continued their heroic efforts, unaware of the emotional storms raging outside their doors.

After six continuous hours of struggle in the operating room, the doctor appeared at the door, his face bearing the signs of exhaustion mixed with a note of relief. He approached Bella's parents with slow, weary steps, as they anxiously awaited any news that could emerge from that white room. Their hands, trembling and intertwined, and the hope glowing in their eyes with each passing second.

Silence reigned for a few moments before the doctor began to speak, his voice laden with the weight of responsibility:

"The surgery was difficult, but I'm glad to inform you that it was successful, and Bella is alright."

He paused for a second, catching his breath, and continued:

"However, she will be moved to the intensive care unit and will need to stay with us for some time under observation."

The anxious expressions on the parents' faces transformed into tears mixed with joy and gratitude as they listened to the news that brought them relief. Bella's father shook the doctor's hand firmly, expressing his deep thanks without finding the right words. Natalie, Bella's mother, struggled to hold back her tears, muttering words of thanks and prayers.

When Emma received the news, she felt like she was breathing for the first time. Upon hearing that Bella had survived and her life had been saved, a wave of relief coursed through her veins, and tears of joy began to flow abundantly, like rain cleansing the earth after a long drought. She felt that life had given her a new chance, an opportunity to cherish every moment she shared with Bella and to be by her side in all that was to come. Her tears transformed from tears of fear to tears of profound gratitude. She resolved never to argue with her sister again, but to be her support and strength.

The doctor stepped aside, giving them time to absorb the news, his gaze filled with deep empathy. A weight lifted from his shoulders, despite the fatigue that still clung to him. His mission had not been just to perform surgery but to fight to restore hope—not only to this family but to all the followers who loved Bella.

In the adjacent intensive care rooms, one housed Bella and the other Daniel, each finding themselves in a tough battle towards recovery. Bella, undergoing treatment for severe injuries, and Daniel, suffering his own pains, shared the journey of healing.

****

In a continuous stream of time, where days blend into weeks without interruption, Bella and Daniel remain confined in the heart of the intensive care unit, like two isolated islands in an ocean of hope and pain. Bella, beginning her journey to recovery, gradually regains her strength, like a leaf slowly unfurling under the warm rays of the sun, taking each new day as another step toward returning to normal life. On the other hand, Daniel, like barren land that hasn't received a drop of rain, remains unchanged, showing no noticeable improvement. Time passed heavily for his sister, with each second feeling like an hour, each hour stretching into a day. Helplessness and despair alternated in visiting her heart.

In a moment that marked the end of one phase and the beginning of another, the doctor stood beside Bella's bed, a slight smile on his face, bearing good news for her and her family.

Silence prevailed for a few moments before the doctor began to speak, his voice laden with the weight of responsibility:

"We are in a very good state. Your condition has improved significantly, and all that remains are some fractures. God willing, we will remove the cast a month from now. I can write you a discharge from the intensive care unit and transfer you to a regular room. You will stay with us for a day or two under observation, and then we can write you a discharge from the hospital. Thank God for your safety, Ms. Bella."

Natalie swallowed a lump in her throat, tears welling up in her eyes, but this time, they were tears of joy and gratitude.

"Thank you, Doctor. Thank you very much. Praise be to God, praise be to God. I can't believe this nightmare is almost over. You can't imagine how worried I was about my daughter, Doctor. Thank you so much, we have troubled you greatly."

"It's no trouble at all, ma'am. This is my duty, and thank God that Ms. Bella is well. I will leave you now to get ready, and I will notify them to prepare a room for your stay in the hospital for follow-up. Excuse me."

As the doctor closed the door behind him, Bella's questions about her husband, James, began to pour out.

"Mom, where is James? Didn't he come to ask about me?"

Her mother took a deep breath, her heart sinking in sorrow for her daughter who kept wondering about a man who never reciprocated her love.

"Forget him, Bella. Focus now on recovering well, getting back to your show. People don't stop asking about you. If you step outside the corridor for a bit, you will find many journalists waiting eagerly for any news about you or the singer in the room next to yours. People love you very much, Bella, and they haven't stopped praying for you."

"A singer in the room next to mine? Who is in a condition like mine?"

"The singer's name is Daniel. My dear, you're fine now, fortunately, but he's not so lucky. He's in a completely different world, in a coma for over a month. You were admitted to the hospital on the same day, but fortunately for us, you'll be released now. May God give his family the strength and patience to endure seeing him in such a state ".

Chapter Three

"Daniel? Oh my God," Bella whispered, her voice trembling. "His wedding was coming up. He and his bride... they were stunningly beautiful. Everyone was amazed by their love." She shook her head in disbelief, her eyes searching for some kind of understanding. "How could this happen?"

Her mother, sitting beside her bed, sighed deeply and rested a hand on Bella's arm. "Nothing stays the same, my daughter," she murmured, her voice soft yet heavy with meaning. "It is impossible for their happiness to continue unbroken like that. Perhaps they were struck by the evil eye."

Bella looked up sharply, the words cutting through her haze of disbelief. "Mom, do you really believe that?" Her tone was gentle but firm. "Everything we see in our lives is destined and written long before we even take our first breath. Each step we take paves the way for the next one. The evil we see now may turn out to be good in ways we don't understand yet. Even if it doesn't seem good on the surface, it will definitely make us stronger."

Her mother's eyes softened, but doubt still lingered in her gaze. "Maybe you're right," she said quietly, her hand tightening slightly on Bella's arm. "But sometimes, it's hard to see the good in the midst of all this pain. It's hard to believe that this, too, is part of some greater plan."

Bella's eyes fluttered shut for a moment, her mind wandering to Daniel—his smile, his charm, the way his voice had captivated the hearts of millions. She couldn't imagine him lying helpless in a hospital bed, his vibrant energy dimmed. "We don't get to choose what happens to us, Mom. But we do get to choose how we react to it."

A long silence settled between them, the weight of their words hanging in the air. Bella felt her mother's warmth next to her, a reminder that no matter what had happened, she wasn't alone. And yet, somewhere deep inside her, Bella knew that things had shifted—life wasn't going to be the same, not for her, not for Daniel, not for anyone.

"I just hope," Bella whispered, "that whatever comes next, we're ready for it."

Her mother nodded, her eyes glistening with unshed tears. "We will be, my daughter. We have to be."

Suddenly, a series of knocks on the door interrupted their conversation, and within a moment, nurses marched into the room with synchronized, steady steps. They gathered around Bella's bed, each holding something that symbolized hope and the excellent care embodied in their profession.

With looks filled with compassion and support, they began preparing Bella to leave the intensive care unit. One carefully handled the covers, another arranged the necessary medications for the transition, while the third helped Bella put on her clothes.

Finally, with everything ready, one of the nurses gently pushed the wheelchair towards the door, heralding the beginning of Bella's journey to her new room. As she was being wheeled out of the intensive care unit, Bella noticed Daniel lying motionless on his bed through the glass of the adjacent room, and she asked the nurse to stop the wheelchair for a moment in front of his room. Bella gazed at Daniel in his deep slumber, realizing deep within that this wouldn't be the last time she saw him.

In a voice full of worry, Natalie asked:

- What's wrong, Bella? Why did you stop here?

- It hurts so much, Mom. That's my favorite star. I wish from the bottom of my heart that he gets well soon.

Natalie patted her shoulders gently and said calmly:

- He will get well, my dear. Come now, let's go to the new room so you can rest.

The nurse continued to steadily push the wheelchair towards the new room while Bella's eyes wandered through the hallways that had witnessed her bitter struggle. The doors opened one by one, not only to other rooms but also to new horizons of hope and opportunities. As she passed through those corridors heading to her new refuge, each step felt like it was pushing her closer to freedom, to a life beyond these four walls. Bella, who had recovered from the most severe stages of illness, now stood on the threshold of a new beginning, full of life. She inhaled deeply, welcoming every breath as a sign of the new life eagerly awaiting her.

The nurses helped her lie down on her bed again. At that moment, her sister, father, and mother gathered around her like guardians of love, standing as her support and shield against the raging storm of conflicting emotions. In her new room, surrounded by walls filled with familiarity and love, Bella stood at the crossroads of heart and mind, teetering between pain and hope. Despite the security that enveloped her in her new room and the embrace of her family, Bella couldn't deny the heavy burden of sorrow weighing on her shoulders. Yet, no matter how deep the pain and intense the betrayal, she couldn't extinguish the faint spark still burning deep in her heart. Her thoughts were tied to Amelia, the man who had filled her life with love and promises before tearing it apart with his betrayal.

The thoughts about the possibility of forgiveness and rebuilding that fractured relationship endlessly swirled in her mind, like a storm that wouldn't calm. Her longing for James, her husband who shattered her heart with betrayal, was like a flood overwhelming her emotions, engulfing every corner of her mind, pulling her away from any attempt at peace.

Emma's warm voice broke through that storm:

- Thank God you're okay, the best sister in the world. I would have died if anything had happened to you .

- Now you know my value. Bella said jokingly.

- What are you saying? Are you going to become arrogant now? I didn't realize your value; I was relieved from your annoyance, and at least no one was taking my clothes from me.

Suddenly, everyone in the room burst into laughter.

With a voice mixing wisdom and kindness, the mother began to explain:

- Oh, Emma, you trickster. Who was the one crying day and night, praying for her sister's recovery?

- Don't worry, Mom. I know Emma is joking.

Emma approached Bella, and with a gesture overflowing with emotion and warmth, she hugged her with a tender, affectionate embrace.

Then, in a voice flowing with longing and yearning, Emma whispered:

- May God never deprive me of you, Bella. You are not just my sister; you are my sister, friend, daughter, and mother.

Bella gently patted her sister's hand, then said with a voice full of emotion:

- May God never deprive me of you either.

Then the mother continued:

- May God protect you for each other, my dear, and protect you from all harm, and may each of you be the best support for the other.

Suddenly, the atmosphere was interrupted by the soft creak of a door opening. James stood on the threshold, a hesitant figure lingering in the doorway like a shadow uncertain of its place. At that moment, every eye in the room slowly turned toward him, casting looks filled with inquiry and wonder.

The silence that descended was heavy and palpable, every breath held in anticipation. What could this unexpected arrival of James mean? Was it a sign of a new beginning or a reminder of a wound that had yet to heal?

As James lowered his head and stepped into the room, shock and confusion gripped the hearts of those present. In those first few moments, it was as though time itself had paused under the weight of surprise. The faces of the mother, father, and sister were marked by mixed expressions of astonishment and questioning, as if the shadows of the cloudy past had seeped into the light of their once peaceful present.

With quiet steps, James moved forward, his presence igniting unspoken tension. The father, catching his wife's eye with a knowing glance, silently decided that it was time for the couple to be left alone. Rising from his seat with a gentle but purposeful motion, he took his wife's hand, exchanged a look of understanding with his daughter, and calmly led them both out of the room, leaving the space for James and Bella to confront whatever lay between them.

In the room, thick with conflicting emotions and unspoken words, James began to speak in a hesitant tone, full of confusion and uncertainty, as if searching for a beginning he had not yet found. His voice, barely louder than a whisper, reached Bella.

"How are you, Bella?"

Bella, battling the flood of tears gathering in her eyes, refused to let them fall. She fought to maintain her strength, but her voice carried all the weight of her pain and confusion.

"Why did you do it? Why did you betray me?"

James's response came in a near whisper, his eyes fixed on the ground as if searching for a place to hide, unable to meet her gaze.

"Because I loved her."

Bella's defenses shattered, and her tears flowed freely as she repeated in agony, "You loved her? How can a heart love two people? Wasn't it you who loved me? Wasn't it you who always told me that? You said you thanked God every day for my presence in your life and that without me, you couldn't go on. So how did you continue with another? How can you say that you loved her?"

James stepped closer, his movements slow and hesitant. He gently took her hands in his and said softly, "Don't cry. I don't deserve these tears. You deserve someone much better than me. It's over, Bella. You are officially divorced now."

When James left the room, it felt as though the echo of a bomb had just exploded, shattering Bella's last remaining hopes. His heavy footsteps through the door left behind nothing but a silence laden with pain and shock, a silence that confirmed the time for regret had long passed, and that harsh reality had now settled deep within her soul. After he left, Bella collapsed under the weight of her tears, and the room itself seemed to drown in her sorrow. Her tears, tracing paths of grief on her face, made every corner of the place appear darker. Bella had clung to a sliver of hope, yearning for James's return to signify a renewal of their vows, a mending of their broken relationship. But with his decision to divorce, he destroyed those hopes.

Bella was ready to overcome the pain of betrayal and heal her wounded pride if James had offered even a slight apology. She was ready to forgive. But with the shock of divorce, all those preparations vanished into thin air, leaving behind a broken heart and a soul seeking solace in her new reality.

When the sound of the door closing behind James echoed, leaving behind the traces of his shocking decision, the family was engulfed in a storm of mixed emotions, prompting them to anxiously head towards the room to discover what had transpired between the couple. They carried a glimmer of hope in their hearts, hoping that James had apologized to Bella to help her through this difficult time she was experiencing. But this hope did not stem from love or a desire for reconciliation; the entire family had never been satisfied with this relationship from the beginning, all aware of the deceitful face James hid, except for Bella, who always looked at him with eyes full of love and hope.

No words were needed; as soon as the doors opened, scenes of pain and heartbreak awaited them. Bella, who had always been a source of strength and optimism, was now crumbling, drowning in her tears that flowed abundantly. She cried in a silence that tore at the soul, the kind of crying that emanates from the depths of a broken heart, carrying with it an overwhelming sorrow.

The family surrounded Bella, offering her support in her difficult moments. Her mother embraced her, her eyes reflecting the tears of sadness and empathy. Her father, with the strength he always had and hid behind his stoicism, stood gently patting her shoulders, trying to be the pillar she needed to stand. Her sister, holding Bella's hand firmly, showed her attempts to offer support and comfort. Continuously twisting in an effort to express her feelings, she asked gently:

- What happened, Bella? Why are you crying like this?

"He divorced me. He came here just to tell me that he divorced me. As if what happened to me wasn't enough because I was already hurt from the past and from his absence when I needed him the most; so he decided to cut me with a cold knife."

Then she broke into sobs and continued:

- I couldn't hate him even after his betrayal. If my heart could hate him, I wouldn't be this broken now. Oh God, give me strength; I am weak.

Emma and Natalie broke into tears, while the father chose to withdraw from the room quietly, heading outside where he could allow his tears to flow away from the eyes of others.

******

In the sterile white room where Daniel lay, the walls echoed with the sounds of medical monitoring devices. Daniel was surrounded by a cluster of machines measuring his pulses and breaths. Every beep from those machines carried a message about his critical state, and every flash of the lights was a reminder of the thin thread of life he was hanging by.

Finally, Violet appeared at the hospital. She came to visit Daniel, where, as a wife, she was expected to be by his side from the very first moment. However, after a month of Daniel's hospitalization, his wife entered the room, her eyes meeting her husband, surrounded by doctors and equipment. She did not wait long in that room which demanded much bravery; everyone in life faces a test of courage, and only a few succeed.

Violet went to the office of the doctor responsible for Daniel's case, knocked on the door, and then entered. Violet did not need to introduce herself to the doctor; in fact, he knew her well from the wedding, which had been shared across all platforms and TV programs. Daniel was the dream boy of many girls and a role model of success for many young men, with a large following. Violet sat on the chair in front of the doctor's desk and immediately asked:

- What about Daniel's condition?

- I won't lie to you, and I don't think words will change the reality. Daniel's chances of survival are slim; every day he remains in a coma brings him closer to death. As of now, we cannot determine the cause of the coma, and there are no visible physical illnesses.

Shock and disbelief filled her eyes. Her steps were heavy, as if she were carrying the weight of the world on her shoulders, as she left the room without uttering the rest of the words stuck in her throat. She couldn't bear to stand there for another moment and left the hospital as if fleeing from a reality she couldn't face. Her sadness was not just about the possibility of losing him but also about what would come after his death. How would she get all his money without sharing it with another heir?

The next day, she returned with more determination in her steps, and her eyes bore a hint of betrayal. She carried a bundle of documents in her arms, papers of renunciation promising to change the course of her and Fares' lives forever. She sat beside him, her gaze cutting through the heavy silence of the room, trying to find any sign in his unconscious state indicating an understanding of what was happening, but she found nothing, which reassured her. Carefully, she began to ink his thumb with blue ink before pressing it lightly on the signature line of the document. With each page turned, she guided his finger to leave his fingerprint on the papers, which promised to transfer his assets to her, thus gradually transferring his possessions to her.

Chapter Four

Only two days had passed when fate cast its heavy shadow on Amelia. Violet visited her at a house that had been a refuge and a repository of memories for Amelia and her late brother. This house, which Daniel had purchased for them without completing the transfer of ownership, saw Amelia open the door to find Violet confidently stepping inside and taking a seat in the nearest chair, adopting a formal posture with one leg over the other, signaling the beginning of an unexpected confrontation.

- How are you, Amelia?

- I'm fine, Violet. Since your return from the trip, no one has seen you. I don't think you've visited Daniel even once. Is everything okay?

- Yes, I'm fine, Amelia. I was just finishing some paperwork.

- Paperwork for what?

- Paperwork for the transfer of ownership. Daniel, my dear, has transferred all his assets to me.

- What are you saying? That's impossible; Daniel could never do that.

- Well, he did. And now I'm here to take my house. Come on, Amelia, get out of here.

- You're going to evict me from my brother's house, Violet?

- I told you, it's no longer your brother's house.

- This is my brother's house, and you're lying. It's impossible that my brother would have transferred anything to you, especially not this house.

- Leave with your dignity rather than being evicted by the police. My lawyer is working on the paperwork, and in two or three days, the police will come to enforce the transfer of my property. By the way, I see Daniel suffering on those machines. The doctors told me there is no hope for him, and the hospital is charging exorbitant fees. We're more deserving of that money.

Tears began streaming down Amelia's face as she said:

- It's impossible for you to be human. You're a devil. How were we deceived by you? How did I see you as my friend? I was the one who welcomed you into my home and introduced you to Daniel, after you had only wished to see him from afar. You got close to me for his sake, using me as a means to come into my home and talk to him. I was the one who made him love you, and in the end, this is what you do to us?!

- Enough. You talk about yourself and what I've done, while Daniel is dying right now. Your many grievances that you've showered upon me are of no value now.

Amelia broke down in tears, saying:

- You have no mercy. Where will I get the money for the hospital? Even if I sell my car and all my jewelry, it won't be enough for more than a week in this hospital. What will I do?

- Remove the machines from him, let him rest and meet his maker, rather than continuing to suffer. Or if you feel guilty, transfer him to a less expensive hospital; the money you have will suffice for that.

Violet sighed and said:

- Out of consideration, I'll give you two days to sort out your affairs. And regarding the hospital expenses, once the ownership transfer is completed, I won't pay a single penny. Either you remove the machines from him or transfer him to a less expensive hospital as I suggested. Goodbye.

Amelia collapsed into a whirlpool of despair and helplessness. Tears flowed endlessly down her cheeks, mingling with the pain of betrayal and disappointment. She thought about Daniel's fate and how his life, hanging by the thinnest threads of hope in the hospital, might end due to the cruelty of fate and human greed.

How would Amelia face the coming days without a home or money, in a world that seemed to be collapsing around her at a terrifying pace? How could she manage the expenses of Daniel's treatment and stay in the hospital, when the house that had once been filled with laughter and hopeful conversations had now turned into a realm of painful silence and deadly solitude? Every corner reminded her of Daniel and Henry, their shared dreams that had evaporated into thin air, the future that might have been.

In this dark moment of her life, she had to find within herself the strength to keep fighting, not only for her survival but also for Daniel, who needed every ounce of strength she could muster. But where does strength come from when everything around you seems to be falling apart? How do you fight when you feel you've already lost everything? With a determination she had never known before, Amelia wiped her tears with the back of her hand, leaving behind the trace of sorrow and despair that had overtaken her for a moment. She moved slowly toward her bedroom, went straight to her jewelry drawer, and gathered all the gold and jewels she had—pieces that held cherished memories and unforgettable moments. But necessity outweighed any memory.

Carrying her jewelry in her arms, Amelia left her home with a firm resolve, heading toward the jeweler her family had dealt with for years. When she arrived at the jeweler's store, he greeted her with a look of concern and sympathy, as he knew the value of these pieces to her and her family. Amelia didn't hesitate, laying all her belongings before him, taking a deep breath as she explained her urgent need for money. The jeweler didn't need much explanation; the sadness in her eyes was enough to tell the story of the desperation that drove her to this action. He assured her that he wouldn't put those pieces up for sale and would keep them until she returned to retrieve them, hoping that her distress would pass.

The jewelry was sold quickly—pieces that meant so much to her, but at this moment, they were just a means to secure Daniel's survival and continue her fight in life. Thus, with steps heavier than those she had taken to leave, Amelia returned home, her hands empty of jewelry but her heart full of resolve and determination to face whatever lay ahead. Carrying her jewelry in her arms, Amelia took confident steps toward the jeweler her family had dealt with over the years. Upon arriving at the store, the jeweler greeted her with a look filled with concern and empathy, understanding the personal and familial value of these pieces. Amelia, without hesitation, laid out her treasures before him, explaining her harsh circumstances with a deep breath. The sorrow etched on her face was enough to convey the tale of the despair that drove her to this decision.

With a human touch, the jeweler promised not to sell the jewelry, assuring her that he would hold onto it, hoping she would return to reclaim it someday, wishing her to overcome this hardship peacefully. The pieces, which had held deep emotional value, had become in that moment merely a means to ensure Daniel's life continued and Amelia's resilience in the face of fate's challenges.

Heading to the hospital, with each step drawing her closer, her heart pounded intensely, unsure if it was fear of losing him or hope that the money would be enough to save his life. She entered the building, now familiar with every corner, heading straight to the accounting department, clutching the money as if it were a final lifeline.

In front of the accounts window, Amelia stood with a mixture of defiance and desperation. She extended her hand, holding the money to the employee, trying to maintain a steady voice as she explained that the funds were for her brother's treatment. Her eyes glistened with suppressed tears, unwilling to show weakness.

When she handed over the amount, she hoped to hear some news that would bring her comfort, but what she received was a shock she wasn't prepared for.

The employee began with a tone that was both sympathetic and firm:

- The amount you've paid, ma'am, has covered the previous charges. We need you to leave an additional deposit to continue the account.

Amelia, with tears streaming down her face and her heart aching, pleaded with the receptionist in a choked voice:

- Please, I don't have any more money. Let Daniel stay in the hospital. I promise you that when he wakes up and recovers, he will repay the hospital expenses himself.

The employee replied with a sympathetic yet helpless tone:

- Believe me, Daniel is beloved by millions, and I'm one of his fans. But there's nothing I can do. If his account isn't settled, they will discharge him.

******

In Bella's room, softly lit and filled with the scent of medication, Bella sat on her bed. Known for her angelic voice and dazzling presence on screen, her heart was now heavy with sorrow and her spirit shattered by the trials she had faced.

She listened to the doctor as he delivered news about her recovery:

- You're in good condition, thank God, and you'll be discharged from the hospital. However, your foot is still not in good shape and will remain in a cast . It's best for you to rest in bed during this time, and you should avoid going to work.

She responded with resignation:

- Alright, Doctor.

Before Bella received her discharge papers, her family was bustling with stress and anticipation that had overshadowed their recent days. But when the doctor informed them of the discharge, the sudden joy replaced the gloom that had weighed heavily on their hearts.

As soon as the doctor left, nurses entered the room to assist Bella with her preparations for departure. One nurse carefully emptied Bella's bedside drawer, gathering personal items like medications, prescriptions, and her mobile phone into a small box. Another nurse folded the clothes that her family had brought during their visits. With all preparations complete and everything ready for departure, Bella, leaning on crutches, took one last look at the room that had witnessed her change and struggle. That moment marked the end of her hospital recovery phase and the beginning of a new journey towards healing and reclaiming her life.

****

The receptionist's words pierced Amelia's, leaving behind a sense of helplessness and frustration. For a moment, she felt as if the ground beneath her was shaking. How could she find more money after having sold everything she owned? Despair began to creep into her soul.

As Bella was heading towards the exit, she overheard a tense conversation between Amelia and the receptionist. The receptionist's tone was asking for more money to ensure that Daniel continued to receive the necessary medical care. The weight of these words seeped into Bella's heart, surprising her and prompting her to help.

In the hospital's expansive reception area, a place filled with souls eager for good news and hearts weighed down by anxiety, Amelia sat alone on one of the long benches. Surrounded by a subtle hum of voices and movement, her internal world sank into painful silence. Her head was slightly bowed, her hands clenching each other with tension and worry, as if trying to grasp the last threads of hope slipping through her fingers.

Tears fell silently down her cheeks, each drop carrying a story of pain, helplessness, and a desperate call for miracles. She tried hard to hide her tears from others, covering them with her hands or wiping them quickly before drawing attention. But these tears were the truest expression of the storm raging inside her heart and soul.

Bella noticed Amelia's state and looked at her with sympathy, but at that moment, she wasn't sure what to do. The morning after returning to her father's home, lying in her room that she had missed, Bella greeted the first rays of sunlight with heavy eyes. Despite the apparent comfort of returning to a place filled with warmth and memories, her comfort was disturbed by thoughts swirling like a hidden storm. She was haunted by the image of Amelia's situation with the receptionist, her strong desire to help, and her own painful experiences with her ex-husband and the decisions she needed to make later. All these matters filled her mind, preventing her from enjoying the tranquility she had longed for.

After moments of reflection, Bella decided to call the hospital administration. She made sure her tone was precise and clear, asking to speak with the hospital director:

"The secretary told me that Miss Bella Philip is on the phone. I couldn't believe it, thank God you're safe, Miss Bella. I've been following your condition daily. Are there any complaints or issues?

"Thank you, Doctor. There are no complaints. You've done everything needed and more. I'm calling about Daniel.

"Daniel the singer, poor thing. We're consulting foreign experts to determine the cause of his coma, but we haven't been able to help him wake up. We've received a notice from the bank about freezing Daniel's account, and as you know, this hospital is private and owned by investors. Unfortunately, I can't keep him here for long. His sister paid part of the bill yesterday, but from what I understand from the receptionist, she doesn't have more to pay.

"I have a personal request. I will transfer a substantial amount to cover Daniel's account for an extended period, but I would like it to remain confidential, so that no one knows, including Daniel when he regains consciousness, or his sister.

"Thank you, Miss Bella. Your kindness is much appreciated. I'll ensure that this information remains strictly confidential."

The conversation was brief and straightforward, and once it ended, Bella felt a weight lift from her chest. She wasn't seeking thanks or recognition; all she wanted was to help Daniel.

Once Bella transferred the amount to Daniel's account, the receptionist eagerly awaited Amelia's arrival, carrying news he hoped would be a balm for her heavy heart and despair. He knew well that Amelia was going through a tough time, surrounded by sadness and drowning in a sea of despair.

When Amelia entered the hospital, the receptionist greeted her with a different tone than usual, accompanied by a warm smile that conveyed hope. She walked toward him, laden with anxiety and tension, expecting him to ask her to find another hospital for Daniel due to her inability to cover the additional treatment costs.

However, she was not prepared for his next words, as he surprised her by saying:

"I have news that will make you very happy. Daniel's account has been covered with a very large amount; there's an anonymous donor, whose identity we don't know, but they paid a huge sum.

Amelia stopped breathing for a moment, her eyes widening in astonishment. The words echoed in her ears like the long-awaited melody. At that moment, she felt the weight of the world lift off her shoulders, and what had seemed like a never-ending dark tunnel was suddenly illuminated by a glimmer of hope.

In that moment, which felt like a small miracle in times when miracles were scarce, Amelia looked up to the sky, overwhelmed with feelings of gratitude and relief. "Thank God," Amelia whispered, feeling the burden lift from her shoulders. Her heart, heavy with worries and fears, began to lighten, and for a moment, she felt that the world still held some goodness.

The receptionist nodded, sharing her sense of satisfaction for the anonymous act of kindness, his eyes shining with compassion and humanity. As Amelia walked away towards Daniel's room, her steps were lighter, and her heart was filled with gratitude. She then thought that Violet had no choice but to leave Daniel in that state and not abandon him.

Amelia took her usual seat next to Daniel since the first day of his hospital stay and began to talk to him:

- Daniel, how are you today?

"I have some good news for you. A significant amount of money has been transferred to your account at the hospital," she said softly, her voice tinged with hope. "I can't shake the feeling that it was Violet who did this. Maybe her conscience got the better of her, and she's terrified of how things will be once you wake up. She must be afraid of losing you, and I don't believe any of it was an act. She loved you, Daniel—truly. What she did, taking your money, wasn't out of malice but out of fear and shock."

She paused, taking a breath as emotions surged through her. "I'm going to see her today. I'll hug her and try to mend things, to bring everyone back together. But... I sold everything, Daniel. I have no home now. I don't know what to do, and I'm lost. I'm hoping—no, I'm counting on you to help me find my way back. You'll give me my home back, won't you? I realized just how much I love you. I miss your jokes, your hugs, and that sense of safety I always felt when you were near."

Her voice trembled as she spoke his name again, hoping against hope that somehow, he could hear her.

In the midst of her exhaustion, Amelia found strength in her unwavering desire to stay by his side. She gazed at him with eyes full of love and care, watching the gentle rise and fall of his chest as he breathed steadily. Taking his warm hand in hers, she traced its familiar lines with her fingertips, as if trying to pass her warmth and reassurance into him. Then, almost instinctively, she rested her head on his hand, surrendering to the fatigue that had steadily overtaken her. And so, beside his bed, she fell asleep, her fingers still entwined with his.

******

Meanwhile, in another home, a very different battle was unfolding. Emma sat on the edge of the couch, her eyes heavy with unspoken words, a silent plea for peace shining through the pain. Opposite her stood Carter, her husband, his face a mask of anger and frustration, as if he were carrying the weight of unspoken grievances.

With a voice strained by weariness, Emma attempted to bridge the growing distance between their hearts. "Why, Carter? Why this treatment? Every day there's another argument about my family, and I still don't understand what they did to you. Since the day we married, my father has tried everything to make you happy."

Carter's expression hardened further as he snapped back, "You really don't know, do you? They treat me like I'm nothing, like I don't belong."

Emma bit back her rising frustration, keeping her tone measured. "I spend most of my time working to give you the life you deserve—the life worthy of Emma Philip, the daughter of a wealthy businessman." She took a small step toward him, closing the distance, and gently grasped his hand. His arm hung heavy at his side, but she held on, looking into his eyes, her voice softening. "All I want is for us to find our way back to each other, Carter."

Then she hugged him, saying:

" I've missed you so much, Carter, I missed the CarterI loved. Don't build bridges between us, as we might lose our way someday.

Carter, indicating that everything he did was for her, replied:

"Bridges? I'm doing all this to please you and to satisfy your family, and to be at a level worthy of you.

Emma answered:

" My dear, my family and I are content with you without all that you do. Just stay with us and be part of our lives.

The truth that Emma tried to hide behind a facade of confidence was that her family indeed did not find anything admirable in Carter , not because of his middle-class status or financial resources, which had never been their concern, but because of Carter's essence. The real obstacle was his rigid personality, his constant neglect of his appearance, along with his heavy demeanor and lack of wit and flexibility in dealing with others, which was further compounded by a certain malice in his behavior that everyone saw clearly except Emma.

With patience and perseverance, Emma tried every possible way to improve James's image in front of her family and those around them.

She immersed herself in attempts to update his wardrobe and encouraged him to develop his communication skills, hoping to see the fruits of her efforts. Yet, time and again, these attempts met with a solid wall of rejection and stubbornness.

Carter, for his part, saw these attempts as a threat to his independence and essence. He did not understand the need for change, clinging to the idea that love should be unconditional and unreserved, ignoring the fact that healthy relationships sometimes require concessions and changes for growth and prosperity. Consequently, the gap between carter and Emma's family continued to widen.

******

AmeliaOverwhelmed with a deep sense of gratitude, Amelia decided to visit Violet that afternoon, convinced that Violet was the benefactor who had deposited money into her brother's account and had saved Daniel. She stood in front of the door to the home that Daniel had lovingly and carefully prepared for them, hesitating for a moment before knocking.

When the door opened, Amelia, with a trembling voice, struggled to hold back her tears as she said:

- I came to thank you for your kindness to Daniel. I know you love him dearly, and he, Violet, loves you very much. He wanted to give you the world and place it at your feet before what happened to us.

- What are you talking about? I don't understand.

- Didn't you transfer a large sum of money to Daniel's hospital account?

Violet, who looked momentarily confused, welcomed Amelia into the house calmly before responding.

- No, I didn't transfer anything. The doctors told me that Daniel is nearing death and that his being on life support in the hospital is no longer useful.

Amelia was stunned by Violet's words, stopping in her tracks, dazed and confused. She tried to gather her thoughts again.

- But... then, who? That was all she could say, staring at Violet with wide eyes.

Amid the confused exchange between Amelia and Violet, suddenly, the tension was broken by the sound of footsteps familiar to Violet but strange to Amelia—footsteps approaching the room from the hallway where they were standing.

A man appeared from one of the hallways leading to the foyer, approaching them with a dignified demeanor and a friendly smile, saying:

- Who has come to visit us, my dear?

He was unfamiliar to Amelia, who looked at him with questioning and surprised eyes.

- Who is this, Violet? Who is this man you've brought into my brother's house?

Violet, looking flustered, replied:

- He's an old friend.

- A friend coming out of the bedroom, Violet?

- My dear, your brother is in his final days, and soon I will be a widow. The truth is, I have neither the desire nor the energy to go to court and file for divorce; it's already settled in the end. It's just a matter of time before everything is over with his passing. So, I've decided to wait. After all, I'm still young, and I have the right to seek my own happiness. Do you really think I will spend the rest of my life mourning him?"

Shock overwhelmed Amelia, making her feel as though the very ground beneath her was shaking. Her tears, which had momentarily been frozen in disbelief, began to flow freely, pouring out like a waterfall of pain and disappointment. She moved toward the door, each step reflecting the depth of the wound that had pierced her heart. With a broken voice, her words nearly drowned in a sea of tears, she said:

- How did we not see your true nature?

She spoke these words without turning back, leaving the place, her sorrow and betrayal echoing in her wake.

Chapter Five

After a period of waiting and anticipation, Bella finally regained her strength. With her recovery complete, she found herself heading back to the hospital that morning. The air gently rustled the leaves, heralding the start of a new day. Bella entered the hospital with confident steps, now familiar with its hallways and rooms. The medical staff greeted her with warm smiles, fully aware of all she had endured. After a brief wait, the moment had arrived to have the cast removed from her leg.

As the procedure concluded and her leg was freed from its constraints, Bella felt a surge of gratitude and renewal. The doctor informed her of the need to attend physical therapy sessions and exercise, but she leaned on her crutches and hurried towards Daniel's room. She didn't want to leave without visiting Daniel, the young man who had touched her life unknowingly. She slipped into his room quietly, her heart beating with mixed feelings of anxiety and hope.

She gently opened the door to find Daniel lying there, seemingly lost in deep and peaceful sleep. She approached him slowly, observing him in silence. The room was filled with the smell of disinfectants, but there was also an air of life and determination. She sat beside his bed, watching him with eyes full of warmth and empathy, and began to speak:

- We've never met, never spoken directly, but I'm a huge fan of yours. Every song you've released has resonated with me at some point in my life, as if you could somehow see or feel exactly what I was going through. I realize, of course, that this connection is something that

often forms between an artist and their fans—where the artist is able
to express through words and emotions what their listeners feel but
can't quite articulate themselves.
In a moment of weakness, she saw it clear,
Another her in his arms, drawing near.
The shadow of betrayal, a dark cloud hovers,
Over a home where love once covered,
If their safety meant nothing to him,
Who will be the one to stand within?
Who'll hold them close in times of need,
Be the comfort, the strength indeed?
"This song, Daniel, was the primary reason I became attached to you
and followed your work closely. When this song was released, it felt
like it was narrating the tragedy I experienced. I had just turned
eighteen, and I was so proud of my father, the prominent businessman
who managed an empire of companies. Every time I visited him at his
company, I felt immense pride, and my heart would light up seeing the
respect and admiration people had for him. My father was the man I
saw as successful in everything—successful at home, in caring for us,
and successful in his work.
One day, I was coming back from school and felt a strong desire to see
and hug my father. You know that feeling, Daniel, when you miss
someone you love even though you've only been apart for a few hours.
I asked the driver to take me to my father's company. I decided to
surprise him by visiting without informing him.
When I arrived at the company, the secretary informed me that my
father was in a very important meeting and was busy. But I didn't want
to go home without seeing him, so I decided to go into his office and
wait there. The office was large and filled with books and papers, but it
also had a feeling of warmth and familiarity.
While sitting and browsing through the books on the shelves, I heard
a notification sound from my father's phone, which he had left on the

desk. Driven by curiosity and without thinking, I looked at the phone screen and saw a new message. The message read:

"I miss you, my love. I'll wait for you tonight at our place."

The number was saved under the name "Mery." My heart stopped, and it felt like the world was spinning around me. That message was a huge shock. Who was this "Mery," sending longing messages to my father? I couldn't fathom that my father—who had always been my role model, my ideal in everything—could be involved in something like this. How could someone who presents himself as perfect to others actually be a traitor?

I put the phone back and decided to act as if I hadn't seen anything. But the image I had of my father changed forever. The moments I spent in the office afterward, waiting for my father to finish his meeting, were some of the hardest moments of my life. When my father came in and smiled at me, I couldn't return his smile with the same innocence and love I had before reading the message. I couldn't even give him the hug I had come specifically to give him.

I left the company that day, contemplating how to handle the situation. Should I confront him with what I saw and read? Or should I keep the peace at home and keep it to myself? I realized at that time that I wouldn't find peace until I saw the truth with my own eyes.

I called the driver under the pretext that I would stay at the company for a while and would return home with my father later. My heart pounded as I walked through the familiar corridors of the company. But this time, everything around me seemed mysterious and strange. I waited in a small café next to the company. The place was quiet and overlooked the main street. I ordered coffee but couldn't bring myself to drink it. My eyes were fixed on the company's door, waiting for my father to come out. Time passed very slowly, and every minute increased my anxiety and tension.

Finally, I saw my father leaving the company. I quickly followed him and took a taxi. I instructed the driver to follow my father's car from a distance, not wanting my father to notice the taxi following him in case he stopped me and I would have to confront him.

The car stopped in front of a building. I saw my father get out of the car and enter the building with confident steps, as if he was familiar with the place. I felt the ground shaking beneath my feet, unable to believe I had reached this moment, the moment when I would see the truth.

I stood away from the building, trying to muster my courage. I had two choices: either to walk away and try to forget everything I had seen or to face the truth and see for myself who "mery" was and what she had with my father. After much thought, I gathered all my strength and decided to enter the building behind my father, fearful of what I might see and confront inside.

After gathering my courage and entering the building, I found myself standing in front of the doorman, who looked at me with the usual question that made my heart race faster, as I prepared to answer him. He asked in a simple tone:

- Where are you going?

His question was simple but weighed heavily on me. Nevertheless, I quickly replied with feigned confidence:

- I'm visiting Mr. Philip, the prominent businessman.

The doorman was reassured by my mention of my father's name and position, indicating that I knew him. Therefore, he had no hesitation in telling me where his apartment was, saying:

- He's on the fourth floor. He just went in, you can catch up with him.

His words drove me to quickly run towards the elevator. When I reached the fourth floor, I slowed my pace and my whole body began to tremble. I was scared of what I would see, as anything I saw would have to be kept to myself. I couldn't hurt my mother or tell her anything. As I approached the apartment door, I stood there, hands trembling, unable to make my decision. I hesitated whether to knock or not. But before I knew it, I was pressing the doorbell. Before anyone could open, I quickly climbed the stairs and hid.

My ears were strained to hear any sound coming from behind the door, and indeed, I heard footsteps approaching to open the door. The shock that pierced my heart, Daniel, was that the person who opened the door was mery, my mother's close friend, the face I had seen many times in our home. At every family gathering, mery was always among the first to be invited. It wasn't just about invitations; she was the first my mother turned to when she was upset and the first she went to confide her worries. I remember a time when my mother complained to her about my father's neglect, and mery would console her, saying: "All men are like that. Don't ruin your life and move on for the sake of your daughters. Your husband is handsome, he's still young, and has a lot of money that makes him desirable to any woman

I was stunned, unable to understand how Mary could have betrayed my mother so cruelly—how she could have been so deceitful and hypocritical, entering our home under the guise of friendship only to destroy it. I tried over and over again to warn my mother, to tell her to distance herself from Mary and to stop telling her about her problems with my father. But every time I spoke, I found myself struggling to express the deep anxiety that was gnawing at me. My mother's repeated questions always carried the same unspoken message: *Why should I stay away from Mary? What reason do you have to turn me against her?*

I couldn't find the right words to explain why my instincts screamed against Mary. Every day, I was torn between the storm raging inside me and the unyielding pressures of the world outside. I knew Mary was treacherous, undeserving of my mother's trust, but I couldn't convince her of that. In the end, I had to endure my mother's scolding, accusations burning deeper into me because she didn't understand why I wanted her to keep her distance from someone she trusted—someone she leaned on. She would say,

"You're just like your father; always pushing people away, wanting to leave me with no one by my side."

Her words wounded me, Daniel. I couldn't defend myself, couldn't make her see the truth. The injustice festered inside me, inflaming my hatred toward Mary. I couldn't hide it. It seeped out in everything I did. Whenever she came over, I would retreat to my room, refusing to greet her. When she spoke to me, I would offer nothing in return. This only heightened the tension between my mother and me. Every day felt like a new battle, our relationship eroding into arguments and misunderstandings.

The tension reached its peak. I knew I couldn't let it continue eating away at me. I had to do something, anything, to release the pain that threatened to consume me. So I decided to confront Mary directly, to lay bare the truth I had uncovered—that she was betraying my mother and carrying on an affair with my father.

When I arrived at her door, I summoned every ounce of courage I had left. I rang the bell, my heart racing. Mary opened the door, and her shock was palpable the moment she saw me. I didn't wait; I didn't need any preamble. I unleashed all the anger and frustration that had been festering inside me for so long.

"I know you're cheating on my mother with my father!" I spat the words at her, my voice shaking with rage.

Her face froze. For a fleeting moment, I felt triumphant. I had exposed her, embarrassed her. But her response came like a thunderclap, shattering every illusion I had clung to. She looked me in the eye, unflinching, and said:

"We love each other. He's madly in love with me, and I'm not afraid of our affair. I'm ready to face the whole world, including your mother."

Her words struck me like a bomb. Everything I had rehearsed, every argument I had planned to throw at her crumbled into dust. I was too stunned to react. Without another word, I turned and walked away, unable to face the full weight of her confession.

When my father found out about the confrontation, everything changed. He left her. Soon after, he came to me, begging that I not tell my mother what had happened. I agreed, though I can't quite explain why. Perhaps it was because, in some twisted way, I felt victorious. I had driven Mary out of his life, protected our family—at least, that's what I told myself.

But inside, I was conflicted. A part of me was proud that I had forced my father to choose, that I had saved our home from the devastation that could have followed if the truth had come to light. Yet, another part of me was shattered. I couldn't shake the sadness that clung to me, knowing that the real truth would hurt everyone if it ever surfaced. This victory, if you could call it that, was bittersweet—a taste I never expected, nor wanted, to experience.

Still, I felt compelled to take a decisive step to protect our home and my mother. I demanded that my father sever all ties between Mary and my mother, ensuring that she never stepped foot in our house again. And so it was.

Mary, who had once been woven into the fabric of our lives, stopped answering my mother's calls. With each failed attempt my mother made to reach her, hope slowly waned until it eventually withered away. As the days passed, Mary faded from our world as though she had never been a part of it.

In those early days, I felt a profound sense of relief, certain that I had succeeded in defending our family, sparing my mother from one of the many "follies of men" that could have torn us apart. Our home settled into an illusion of peace—at least, that's what I thought.

But as the years went by, as I grew older, I uncovered a more painful truth about my father. His infidelity hadn't ended with Mary. He continued chasing after younger women, flitting from one affair to the next with shocking ease. When I learned of this, the pain cut deep, yet it also solidified my resolve. I would protect our home, and most importantly, protect my mother—the kindest, most loving woman I had ever known.

To this day, I have remained steadfast in my decision, defending our home and shielding my mother from the heartache that my father's whims could cause. I've always kept a vigilant eye on him, ensuring that his endless desires don't spill into our lives. Even now, Daniel, I am afraid to confront him. Afraid to admit that I know Mary was not an isolated affair, but merely one in a long line of betrayals. Afraid to expose the countless whims that seem to know no bounds.

But enough of that. I didn't come to burden you with my troubles, artist. I'm sorry. I lost track of time while I rambled on. I came to check on you, to see how you were. Goodbye, Daniel. Stay strong. You are stronger than you know.

Bella left the hospital, her steps measured and deliberate, as though each one allowed her to reclaim a piece of herself. Slowly, the confident air of the broadcaster returned, carrying with it a tangled web of emotions. Beneath it all, she felt a faint note of joy reverberating deep within her soul, like a delicate melody being played just for her.

Although she received no response from Daniel and was uncertain if he felt anything around him, she found herself enveloped in an unparalleled sense of peace. This peace felt like a warm embrace on a cold night, a refuge granting her reassurance and stability in a turbulent world. She bid him a temporary farewell, feeling that she would return again, and went back to her father's home, where she had been staying since her separation.

When Bella noticed the light seeping from under Emma's room door, she cautiously opened it to find Emma at her father's house. Bella deduced that Emma's presence here was the result of a recent argument with carter. She expected the atmosphere to be calm, but what she found was entirely different. The silence of the room was pierced by muffled sobs, with Emma sitting on her bed, collapsed among the pillows, tears streaming down her cheeks as she struggled to suppress a violent bout of crying.

Bella asked with heightened concern as she approached her sister, placing her hand on her shoulder in an attempt to offer some support:

- What's wrong, Emma?

Emma's response came in broken gasps as she tried to pull herself together, but her reddened eyes and exhausted face told a different story:

- Nothing, nothing...

Bella, with her insight and knowledge of her sister's relationship with her husband, was able to read between the lines, realizing that the root of the problem was carter once again:

- Is it carter again? What did he do this time?

Emma, who for a moment seemed on the verge of keeping her thoughts hidden, could no longer contain the flood of emotions. Her voice trembled with a mix of frustration and pain as she finally broke her silence. "Carter... it's always about Carter," she confessed, her eyes filling with tears. "I can't keep living like this. Every day, there's something new—another reason to question why I stayed. Today, he hit me because I asked him to work with my father." She paused, her voice wavering, caught between the love she still harbored and the anger that twisted inside her. "I'm going to ask my father for a divorce. But the worst part?" She hesitated, her gaze dropping as she admitted the truth that tormented her most. "I still love him, Bella... God help me, I do."

Bella, who until then had been trying to maintain her composure and offer support, felt anger rising within her, mixed with an indescribable disappointment:

- Get up, Emma! You deserve so much better than him. Why are you enduring all this suffering?

Her voice rose, unable to hide her anger and sadness at her sister's situation. Emma, in turn, between her tears and the aching of her heart, found only defensive counterattacks:

- And you? Advise yourself first. Have you managed to forget James, Bella?

Her words cut through Bella's attempt to stay calm, reminding her of her own wounds.

After Emma's words struck Bella's heart like a thunderbolt, she withdrew from the room in complete silence. Bella found herself unable to respond to Emma; any words spoken at that moment would only deepen the wound. Emma, on her part, felt a pang of regret after unleashing those words and attempted to plead for Bella's forgiveness, but to no avail.

Bella entered her room, closing the door gently behind her. This act was like shutting a gate between her and the noise of the world beyond these walls. In her solitude, she allowed herself a soothing bath. Sleep, this gentle refuge, seemed like the only comfort she could find at that moment. With her eyes closed, Bella let herself drift away from reality, hoping that the morning would bring her some solace.

With the dawn, Bella awoke to a new day. After changing her clothes, she felt an inexplicable urge to step outside, to breathe in the fresh air, and to seek a moment of clarity in this chaotic world.

Almost instinctively, she found herself heading towards Daniel. She wasn't entirely sure why she chose him; perhaps she was looking for someone who wouldn't judge her choices, a chance to express herself without expecting a response, or maybe she was seeking an escape, a way to release everything inside her without shame. But in her heart, she felt that Daniel, despite his condition, might be the only refuge capable of giving her a moment of peace.

In that quiet, white room, Bella sat beside Daniel's bed, which was submerged in a deep coma. The machines emitted their regular beeps, as if trying to fill the heavy silence that hung over the room. With tear-filled eyes and a heart burdened with pain, Bella began to speak to Daniel:

- Daniel, I know you can't respond, but I need to talk. I need to tell someone what's inside me, and you're the only one I can be completely honest with. I don't know why, maybe because I'm sure you can't hear me, so I don't feel ashamed in front of you.

She sighed deeply, trying to gather her thoughts and calm herself before continuing.

- Emma, my little sister, reproached me about my husband who betrayed me. I used to advise her to leave her husband who always made her life miserable and upset her, and that she deserved better than him. She told me:

"You should advise yourself first."

A tear slipped from her eye, followed by another, as memories of the days when Amelia had embodied love and warmth overwhelmed her.

"I don't know what to do," she muttered, her voice unsteady.

"Sometimes, I wonder if I could have made a better choice—the choice to forget, to cut James out of my life forever—but a part of me still loves him. Yet, Emma's words... they cut so deeply. I can't even blame James anymore; I've become the source of my own pain."

She paused, drawing in a shaky breath before wiping her tears away with the back of her hand.

I once told my audience that one of the keys to happiness is choosing someone who brings out the best version of ourselves. But now, I don't see that happening in my own life. I give this advice to others, but I couldn't follow it myself. My heart still loved him despite everything, and I ignored my mind, which constantly warned me: No, don't choose him. Now, I was left to face the worst version of myself because of it.

She calmed down a bit, and her voice softened. "Do you remember, Daniel, the song you once sang, the one where you said..."

In the chaos of the world, I found you,

And I wagered everything on you, too.
I gave you my heart, hoping you'd be mine,**
Your presence alone lit up my entire life.**
They all said, "He's not the one," but I didn't care,
I told them, "What's the right one, then?" I swear.
His love was enough to make my world bright,
But now it's shattered, and nothing feels right.
You confirmed their words and turned away,
You betrayed my heart, leaving me in dismay.
I thought you were my safe haven, my peace,
But in truth, you were nothing more than a fleeting breeze.
The dream I built crumbled in a single night,
They said, "We warned you," and I had no fight.
I lived a love story, its moments so sweet,
But in the end, all I'm left with is regret so deep .

Bella looked at Daniel's motionless features and began to share her story with him, her voice carrying a blend of nostalgia and pain.

- The first time I saw James was at university, and it was a day I will never forget. James, always elegant, with a smile that captivated everyone, seemed like someone straight out of a fairytale. Tall and strikingly attractive, he drew the eye with his beauty before reaching the heart. Despite my father providing us with everything and me always feeling like a princess, James had a special allure, as if no other man existed in the world. I watched him daily as he stood with many girls in a conspicuous manner, and even though I felt my love for him from the very first moment I saw him, I deliberately ignored him, as my pride dictated that.

But perhaps fate had unforgettable moments and dreams waiting to come true for me at any given moment. It wasn't just an ordinary day when my father, Philip, walked in with a smile and told me that he had spoken to a friend of his, the owner of a TV channel. His friend had agreed to let me be a presenter on the channel, giving me the chance to prove myself. His words echoed in my mind, and I felt that this was the beginning of a great opportunity to showcase my talent.

I left university for a whole month, busy with preparations, working on the program that would be aired for the first time. The days flew by between rehearsals and preparations, until the big day arrived. I found myself in front of the camera, under the lights, feeling distinguished, as if I had been born anew.

When I returned to university after this absence, things felt as if I had entered an entirely new world. Everyone was surrounding me to take pictures. I was astonished by the change that had occurred. I hadn't thought about fame before, but it came and brought with it both beautiful and challenging things. I learned at that time that people gather around you when you have some money, but when you have money and fame, the crowd around you increases. I realized that my circle had greatly expanded, but not just in numbers; it was filled with people's hidden desires around me, eager to benefit from my fame. And on that day, James came. I remember well how he walked in with confidence and navigated around me steadily, as if he knew exactly where he belonged in the crowd. His steps were those of someone who had great self-assurance. When he reached my side, he extended his hand to shake mine, with a look of admiration and appreciation I hadn't seen from him before.

James told me with a voice full of sincerity and admiration:

- The show was fantastic, and you were the epitome of beauty and brilliance.

His words flowed like clear water, quenching the thirst within me. I had waited for this moment for so long. For the first time, I felt James saw me. I couldn't hide the joy that filled my heart. The media, which I once thought was just a job I loved and wanted to excel in, became the bridge that brought me closer to James. The moment I had once thought was far away became a reality. The smile on my face was not just a reaction to his words but a reflection of feelings that began to emerge from within me. That day, many things changed, and I understood that life can surprise us with the most beautiful gifts at the simplest moments, and when hearts draw close to each other, anything becomes possible.

Bella sighed, her eyes reflecting a shimmer of sadness.
- I thought I had found true love, a partner who would stand by me through everything. But life had other plans.
I was ready to face the entire world to be with him. Everyone saw him as a cheater chasing after women, except me. On a day I can never forget, my father Philip walked into the room and locked the door behind him. He wanted to talk to me and was afraid someone might overhear what he was about to say. He wanted to prevent my marriage to james by any means. He sat beside me on the bed, looked at me, and began to speak with a voice filled with reverence and pain:
- My daughter, don't be like your mother. A man who has the nature of infidelity, it becomes an addiction to him, he cannot stop. You'll say he cheats because he doesn't love his wife. I'll tell you no, he might love his wife, but the feeling of being desired all the time and women pursuing him, over time turns into an addiction, like drugs.
Sitting beside me, I saw in his eyes an ocean of pain and sorrow, his face revealing more than a thousand words. With a trembling voice and eyes filled with apology, every word he spoke seemed to come from deep within. The words were coming out with difficulty, as if he was speaking about himself, but he wanted to protect me.
I saw in his eyes things I had never seen before, filled with hope and fear, Philip's fear of a future that might be fraught with difficulties. He spoke about his weakness with bravery, bravery I hadn't expected. My heart was breaking seeing the strong man I had known all my life exposing his vulnerability in this way, all to protect me.
Men's qualities are truly strange, Daniel. If each man could view things from this perspective and treat his wife the way he would want his

own daughters to be treated by their husbands, life would be much more beautiful, and there would be no problems between spouses.

Despite all the warnings and advice, my heart clung to the idea of marrying James. Even with all the talk I heard, I was determined. I saw something in him that no one else could see, or maybe I was ignoring what everyone was trying to show me. In my mind, the clear idea at that time was, "As long as he loves me, he cannot betray me."

In short, I chose to follow the path I had set for myself, believing that the love between James and me would be enough to overcome any differences. During the first year of our marriage, it was one of the happiest times of my life—full of joy, happiness, and indescribable beauty. But gradually, things began to change. I started noticing that James would get up from beside me in bed after he thought I had fallen asleep. Sometimes, I would hear him talking on the phone with a woman late at night. Over time, he stopped sleeping next to me altogether. He would spend the entire night out of the house, and I had no idea where he was or what he was doing.

I felt that james was no longer with me; he became distant even when he was close. A woman truly feels her husband, and I felt everything happening, but a part of me was ignoring it, Daniel, ignoring it because it did not want to face the truth. I was afraid that if I faced it, I would have to end it myself, and that was the hardest part.

I ignored many things, clinging to the happiness I had experienced in the first year, hoping that God would guide him back to me so we could continue our lives together. But the truth was approaching gradually, and my heart knew that the end was looming. One day, I had a photo shoot scheduled that would go late into the night, so I told James that I would return in the morning. But fate seemed to have other plans. I finished the shoot a little early and decided to return home. When I arrived, I found the bedroom door slightly ajar and heard laughter and whispers seeping from inside the room.

I opened the door and entered, and the scene that greeted me was harsher than anything I could have imagined. James, whom I had thought was the love of my life, the person for whom I had defied the whole world, was there betraying the trust and love we had shared. I felt as though my heart was going to stop from the shock and pain.

His betrayal outside the home was not enough; he had brought another woman to share in betraying me on our bed, our bed that had once held us in moments of hope and love.

I was frozen in place, unable to believe what was happening, and every beautiful memory of our marriage was unraveling before my eyes. Believe me, Daniel, when I opened the door and saw my husband with another woman on the bed, there was no sign of remorse on his face; he was trying to justify his actions with meaningless words. It seemed in his eyes as if he could not believe that this moment had finally come, as if he was waiting for a chance to give me a reason to end everything between us.

I didn't know what to do; a part of me was screaming, crying, and wanting to smash everything around me, but at the same time, there was a silent part, unable to comprehend what was happening. That day was a turning point, not just the end of a relationship, but a moment when my heart shattered into a thousand pieces.

After leaving the house, I walked barefoot in the streets, not knowing where to go, as if someone had hit me on the head. The tears that filled my eyes were like a flood, making it impossible to see clearly. Strangely, Daniel, the car that hit me was not visible at all. Suddenly, I woke up and found myself here, in the room next to yours. I never expected that life would bring me to you in a place like this and that I would find a friend to talk to. I was in dire need of someone to talk to, Daniel.

After all this pain, I couldn't bring myself to hate James. There was a part of me that tried to remember the beautiful days and move beyond the pain. But what made me truly hate him was not just his betrayal or the pain he caused me; it was something else entirely.

I spent time in the hospital after the incident, and James never came to see me, not even once. He didn't ask about me, didn't care to Know what happened to me. And when he finally decided to come, he didn't come to check on me or to say a kind word; he came to divorce me. That was the final blow. All the love I felt, all the hope for reconciliation, vanished in an instant. I was shattered more than I had ever been, wounded more than I had ever been, and on top of all that, I was alone. The person who was supposed to be by my side in my hardest moments chose to be the cause of my greatest pain.

At that moment, the pain settled in my heart, It wasn't just because he betrayed me, it was because he left me when I needed him the most. He broke the promises we made, and it was all over.

- Oh God, I've troubled you as usual, Daniel. I don't know, but I feel at ease when I'm here, even with the sound of these machines. I'll leave now, though I feel I'll be back soon.

She then gently touched Daniel's hand before leaving the room, which had become a second home to him over the past few days. In a barely noticeable response, Daniel's hand stirred slightly before settling back into the calm stillness he had grown accustomed to. As if echoing the emotional weight of the moment, the surrounding machines emitted a series of unusual sounds, hinting at a surge of abnormal activity as if they were pulsing with life in response to that fleeting touch. However, the disturbances quickly faded, and the machines resumed their steady, rhythmic hum.

As Bella made her way to the hospital's main entrance, she saw Amelia talking to the receptionist, so she approached and stood beside her, pretending to inquire about lab work schedules, a flimsy excuse to overhear the conversation between Amelia and the receptionist:

Amelia stood in front of the hospital reception desk, her eyes filled with anxiety, like clouds before a storm. The receptionist behind the desk looked up at her, trying to offer support with a look of sympathy. "I know this is hard, but... my brother isn't showing any improvement. I'm also worried that the money might run out while he's still in this condition."

The receptionist replied, in a professional tone:

"I understand your concern, Miss Amelia. But please consider once more. Transferring to another hospital at a lower cost might affect the quality of care he receives and negatively impact his condition.

Amelia responded with a choked voice:

"But I'm scared... Scared that the donated funds will run out and my brother will still be in a coma with no improvement. I really don't know what to do.

Amelia started to cry, her eyes filled with confusion as she didn't know where to begin.

Bella intervened and began to introduce herself to Amelia:

"I think I've seen you here at the hospital before. What's your name?

"I'm Amelia Robert.

Then Bella gently patted her shoulder and invited her to have a cup of coffee at the nearest café:

I remember now. You're related to the artist Daniel, aren't you? Bella pretended not to recognize her.

- I'm his sister.

- And what did you study?

- I graduated in Business Administration.

- Can you tell me what happened to him that led to this situation?

Amelia began to recount everything Daniel had gone through, explaining the deep shock caused by their younger brother's death. She described the traumatic incident Daniel couldn't overcome, which eventually led him into a deep coma. Amelia also detailed the betrayal and infidelity he suffered from his wife, noting that he still didn't know about her infidelity. She expressed her fear that he might find out when he wakes up, which could plunge him into an even worse mental state.

As Bella listened to Daniel's story and what he had endured, she felt a wave of emotions growing towards him. She wasn't sure if it was because her own suffering resonated with his or because she was becoming emotionally connected to him. Bella had experienced a similar type of suffering from Daniel , which made her reflect on how trials shape individuals and their characters. Ultimately, Bella felt a deep sympathy for Daniel and began to emotionally connect with his story and experiences.

Bella bade farewell to Amelia with a suspicious glance and left, heading towards her father's office at the company. She carried with her the burden of worry and concern. She entered the spacious and elegant office where her father sat behind his desk, surrounded by work papers and files.

Bella spoke softly:

"Good evening, Dad.

He looked up from his reports with a warm smile:

"Good evening, Bella. Please, have a seat. How was your day?

She sat down in the chair in front of his desk, took a deep breath before starting to speak:

"It was good, thank you. I wanted to talk to you about an important matter.

He set aside the reports and focused his attention on her:

"Of course, what's the matter?

With a bit of hesitation, she twisted her fingers around the edge of the chair:

"I have a close friend named Amelia. She's in a difficult situation right now, and her brother needs very expensive treatment.

He frowned slightly with sympathy:

"That's unfortunate. How can I help?

She gathered her courage, looked into her father's eyes with confidence:

"I thought we could offer her a job at our company with a substantial salary to help cover her brother's medical expenses. But I want it to be done without her knowing that the job was arranged.

He thought for a moment, then nodded in understanding:

"I see. You want it to appear as if she got the job based on her skills and qualifications.

Bella smiled with relief:

"Exactly. She doesn't feel comfortable with donations and always fears they might stop at any moment. I want her to feel secure about covering her brother's treatment continuously without worry.

With a satisfied smile, he leaned forward, resting on his desk:

"I'm proud of you, Bella. I'll arrange it. We'll offer her a good job with a respectable salary, and she will never know it was you behind it.

She breathed a sigh of relief, her eyes shining with gratitude:

"Thank you, Dad. I truly appreciate it.

With affection, he patted her hand:

" No thanks are necessary. The important thing is that we help those in need as much as we can. Provide the secretary with details about the girl, such as her phone number and the university she graduated from, and they will contact her to arrange a suitable job for her.

Bella approached her father and placed her hand on his in appreciation. He patted her hand gently, and returned to his reports with a reassuring smile on his face. Bella left the office with a smile of satisfaction and reassurance.

Chapter Six

Bella entered the hospital in a state of complete breakdown. Her face was pale, her eyes swollen from constant tears. Unable to bear the weight of the pain that shackled her heart, she sought solace in Daniel, hoping that somehow, even in his coma, he would feel her presence. She sat beside him, gently holding his hand, drawing strength from his stillness. Her voice trembled as she began to speak, eyes filled with tears.

"Daniel, I can't bear this pain anymore. I can't stand seeing James happy with his new wife while I suffer alone. I've tried to convince myself I've moved on, that I no longer love him, but every time I go back to our old house, I see him from afar, and the happiness in his eyes... it's like my heart is breaking all over again."

Her words were fractured, carried on sobs and the torment of her heart. She took a deep breath, trying to steady herself before continuing.

"I know I'm hurting myself, but I can't stop. I sit in my car for hours, waiting for him to come out, hoping to catch a glimpse of him. I wish to see even a hint of sadness, something to show me he misses me. But every time I see him with his wife, I see the happiness that used to be mine, and it breaks me, Daniel. It completely breaks me."

There was no response from Daniel, but Bella continued speaking, her voice a desperate plea to his sleeping heart.

"I'm drowning in sadness, Daniel. Every moment reminds me of him—the dreams we built, now shattered, haunting me like nightmares. And I... I've begun to live through the lyrics of the song you used to sing. Every word feels like it was written for me, for the pain James left behind."

She paused, her eyes searching his face for any flicker of acknowledgment. His expression remained unchanged, but she held his hand more tightly. "Do you remember the words of the song I sang last year?" Bella began to softly recite the lyrics.

I wish I could forget you and move along my way
But your shadow remains, haunting me night and day
Memories of the past spin inside my mind
Like knives, they cut deep, leaving scars behind
Oh, heart's wound, so hard to erase
With every moment, the sorrow's embrace
Oh, my pain, oh, my yearning inside
How can I forget, how can I find time's tide?
You were my dream, my life, my guiding light
Now you're just a memory, increasing my plight
Each time I see happiness in your eyes
The pain in my heart knows no goodbyes

"I never imagined that those lyrics would one day reflect the anguish I'm feeling now. That song has become a heartbeat in my chest, a constant reminder of James' betrayal and the lies that haunt me."

Her voice faltered, but she pressed on, hoping her words could somehow reach him.

"Please, Daniel, hear me. I need you to feel my pain, to know how much I'm hurting."

Her gaze softened as she continued, her voice now filled with empathy. "I understand why you're here. The pain of separation from your brother must have been unbearable. You've always had such a tender heart, Daniel. I wish we could talk, support each other through this suffering."

She lingered beside him, her words hanging in the air as she watched him with a mixture of love and sorrow.

Amelia, overwhelmed with concern, left her office at midday and rushed to the hospital. She found Bella at Daniel's bedside, her presence marked by a quiet determination to awaken him from his coma. Observing them for a moment, Amelia was puzzled by Bella's deep distress and the connection she seemed to have with Daniel. She didn't know Bella well, but her curiosity was piqued.

Quietly, Amelia exited the room and made her way to the hospital administration, determined to uncover the identity of the secret donor who had been contributing large sums to Daniel's account. Despite her persistence, she was met with firm refusals due to privacy policies.

Refusing to give up, Amelia returned to Daniel's room and waited until Bella left. She followed her discreetly and watched as Bella made another sizable deposit into Daniel's account. The realization hit Amelia like a shock—Bella was the anonymous donor.

Confusion and astonishment swirled in Amelia's mind. She barely knew Bella, yet this woman was making such generous contributions to Daniel. Why? Was there a hidden connection between them?

Amelia's determination to uncover the truth only deepened.

Before delving further into her investigation, Amelia visited Daniel's doctor for an update on his condition.

"Doctor," she asked, concern etched on her face, "how is Daniel? Is there any progress?"

The doctor offered a reassuring smile. "His vital signs are stable, and physically, he's in good condition."

Amelia frowned in confusion. "Then what's keeping him in a coma? Could it be psychological?"

The doctor nodded. "That's our belief. Emotional trauma can sometimes trigger such conditions. Interestingly, we've observed that Daniel's vital signs improve when Bella speaks to him. Her presence seems to have a positive impact."

Amelia's eyes widened in surprise. "Bella's visits are helping him?"

The doctor smiled gently. "Yes, her presence has become an unexpected form of medicine. We believe continued visits from her could aid his recovery."

Though relieved, Amelia's mind remained occupied with questions. What was Bella's connection to Daniel, and why was she so devoted to helping him?

With her mind full of unresolved mysteries, Amelia left the hospital, determined to find answers and ensure her brother's recovery. But as she returned to work, one thought echoed in her mind: What secret was Bella hiding?

Amelia began her investigation with calm precision, utilizing every resource at her disposal. She delved into every aspect of Bella's life—her family, their history, and their thriving business empire. It didn't take long for Amelia to discover that Bella came from a highly influential family, with a prestigious company and a father who was both respected and powerful in society. Bella was more than just a successful broadcaster; she was part of a family with deep roots and considerable sway.

But gathering information wasn't enough for Amelia. She needed to understand Bella intimately, to truly embed herself within the fabric of Bella's life. Slowly, she worked her way into their circle, forging connections, cultivating friendships, and engaging with Bella's family. Each conversation, every visit, was a deliberate step toward her goal. Amelia was patient and intelligent, knowing that winning Bella's trust would take time.

Soon, her presence became a regular part of their daily lives. She visited their home frequently, joining Bella and her sister Emma in conversations that revealed glimpses of their personal world. Bit by bit, Amelia collected pieces of the puzzle, focusing on Bella's motivations and her mysterious generosity towards Daniel. Amelia was convinced there was a secret buried beneath Bella's actions, and with each passing day, she felt closer to unearthing it.

One afternoon, while the two women chatted in the elegant living room of Bella's parents' house, Bella turned to Amelia with a warm smile.

"Amelia," Bella began softly, "it feels like you've become part of our family. I can't tell you how much our friendship means to me."

Amelia smiled back, her voice gentle. "I feel the same, Bella. I've found such comfort and security with you and your family."

As they shared the warmth of their newfound bond, Amelia couldn't suppress the question that had been nagging her for some time. She hesitated briefly before asking, "Bella, do you mind if I ask you something personal?"

Bella's expression softened, her eyes gentle. "Of course, Amelia. Ask me anything."

Amelia took a deep breath. "I was wondering about your romantic life."

For a fleeting moment, Bella's expression changed, a shadow crossing her face. Her voice grew quieter. "I was married to someone named James. But... we're separated now."

Amelia felt a surge of sympathy. "I'm so sorry, Bella. That must have been incredibly difficult."

Bella nodded, her eyes glistening with unshed tears. "It was. At first, I couldn't believe it, but eventually, I had to face the truth. James cheated on me, and everything fell apart. It was painful, but my father... he supported me through it. He arranged for me to work as a presenter on a European channel, and now I'm focusing on rebuilding my life."

Amelia listened intently, her mind racing. She remembered the doctor's words—how Daniel's condition had been improving because of Bella. The thought of Bella leaving now stirred unease within her. What would happen to Daniel if Bella left? Could his health deteriorate again? Unsure of how to navigate this delicate situation, Amelia resolved to speak with the doctor the next day. Bella's departure might help her heal, but it could also have devastating consequences for Daniel.

Bella smiled softly, a glimmer of hope shining in her eyes, and then she continued in a calm voice, "I think what I really need is a fresh start... to leave James and everything he put me through behind."

As soon as Amelia left Bella's home, her mind was in turmoil. She didn't know how to protect her brother from the potential heartbreak that Bella's departure might bring, but she knew she had to find a way to shield him from further pain.

Chapter Seven

The next morning, the first rays of sunlight quietly crept into the city, as if they were watching what would unfold on this day filled with life-altering decisions. Amelia awoke early, feeling a subtle tension urging her to move quickly. It wasn't just a fleeting sensation; deep down, she knew the time had come to take serious steps for her brother Daniel.

She dressed quickly and left the house, inhaling the crisp morning air. The streets were almost empty at this early hour, allowing her to move freely towards her destination: the hospital. Amelia ran, ignoring the cold seeping into her body, heading to meet the doctor who might hold the answers she needed.

But when she arrived at the hospital, she found that the doctor had not yet come. Frustration coursed through her body like a heavy weight she couldn't shake, but she forced herself to wait. She sat in the waiting room, trying to remain calm as her thoughts revolved around her brother.

In those moments of anticipation, there was another figure moving through the hospital corridors: Bella. This was her final goodbye to Daniel before her departure. Bella approached Daniel's room slowly, her heart weighed down by a mixture of emotions: sadness, fear, and a faint hope that this was not the end.

She entered the room quietly, just as she had done the previous time. Daniel was still lying there, motionless, as if trapped in a world of his own. Bella approached and sat beside him, gently taking his hand as she had done before. She spoke softly, saying:

"Daniel, I came to say goodbye... I'm about to leave. My father insisted that I distance myself from everything that happened here, and maybe he's right."

Her words came out with difficulty, as if she was resisting the urge to cry. But Daniel did not move. There was no response; silence ruled. Bella kissed Daniel's forehead for the last time, as if bidding him a final farewell. She rose from the chair and headed towards the door. The moment of parting was filled with sorrow, but Bella knew this step was necessary for her. She had to start a new life, even though part of her didn't want to leave.

Outside Daniel's room, Bella headed straight to the airport. She had decided to turn off her phone, unwilling to receive any external contact. Bella knew that her decision would not be easy, but she was convinced it was the best choice for herself and her future.

As Bella made her way to the airport, Amelia was still at the hospital, anxiously waiting for the doctor to arrive. With every passing minute, she felt time slipping away, and a sense that something significant was happening beyond her sight. Finally, the doctor arrived. Amelia felt a slight relief as she saw him enter the hospital wing. She quickly approached him, as if eager to get all the answers immediately.

"Doctor, I'm here to ask about my brother Daniel's condition. I've heard that he responded somehow to Bella's visit, and I'm worried that if she leaves, his condition might deteriorate again."

The doctor was calm as always. He looked at Amelia with eyes full of deep thought and said:

"Amelia, in cases like this, it's difficult to determine what's happening in the patient's subconscious mind. Daniel may be responding to certain external stimuli, such as Bella's voice or presence, but we cannot definitively say how much that impacts his recovery. The subconscious is a mysterious area, and her presence might be contributing to his improvement, but it could also be the opposite."

The doctor's words echoed through Amelia's mind. "What if Bella leaves? What if Daniel's condition worsens again?" These thoughts raced in her head. She couldn't wait any longer.

Amelia decided she needed to speak openly with Bella. Bella needed to know the truth, to understand that her visits might be the reason for Daniel's improvement, and that her departure could harm him. Amelia called Bella, knowing when she was supposed to leave and hoping to stop her before it was too late. But Bella's phone was off. Amelia left the hospital, heading to Bella's house, only to discover that Bella had already left. She was overwhelmed by mixed feelings of frustration and despair. She rushed to the airport, but by the time she arrived, Bella was already gone.

But what happened was beyond anyone's expectations. The moment Bella left Daniel's room, it was as if a force inside him refused to let her go. His eyelids fluttered, and with a slow, deliberate movement, Daniel woke from his coma. It was as though he had been fighting to return from the depths of his unconsciousness, driven by an inexplicable urge to stop her departure.

At The airport, Amelia's phone rang, the shrill sound cutting through the tense air. Her heart raced as she answered the call, only to hear the words she had been longing for but never expected to come so suddenly.

"Miss Amelia, your brother... Daniel has woken up. He's come out of the coma."

The world around her seemed to blur as she absorbed the words. For a moment, everything felt suspended in time. Her breath caught in her throat, her mind spinning with disbelief. Then, as if some invisible dam broke within her, relief, joy, and shock surged through her all at once. Tears welled in her eyes, but she didn't have time to let them fall.

Amelia rushed to the hospital, her legs moving almost automatically, fueled by the overwhelming mix of emotions she couldn't fully comprehend. Fear lingered beneath her joy—fear that it was all a mistake that something might change by the time she arrived. Yet hope, that fragile and persistent thing, pushed her forward. Her heart pounded in her chest, each beat heavy with the weight of anticipation.

As she neared the hospital, her mind flooded with memories of Daniel—how he had been before the coma, his laughter, his strength. She clung to the thought of him as she once knew him, praying that this wasn't just a fleeting miracle.

Entering the hospital, she barely noticed the familiar surroundings. Everything was a blur as she hurried through the corridors, her breath quickening with every step. When she reached his room, she hesitated for a brief second, afraid of what she might find, yet desperate to see him awake.

The door creaked open, and there he was—Daniel. His eyes were open, his face pale but alive, no longer trapped in the lifeless slumber that had held him prisoner for so long. His gaze was unfocused at first, but when he saw her, something in his expression shifted—recognition, warmth, the faint flicker of the brother she had been praying to see again.

Tears streamed down Amelia's face as she approached him, every emotion she had suppressed pouring out. She reached for his hand, her touch trembling, afraid he might slip away again. But his fingers curled weakly around hers, and the warmth of that simple gesture sent a wave of reassurance through her.

"Daniel..." her voice broke, but she didn't need to say anything more. The mere sight of him awake, of him being there with her, was enough to fill the void of countless sleepless nights and unanswered questions. In that moment, everything else faded away—the fear of losing Bella, the uncertainty of the future. All that mattered was the fragile connection between them, the bond that had endured despite the odds.

She began speaking with him.

- Daniel, how are you?

In a trembling voice, Daniel asked:
- Where is my little brother?
There was no satisfactory answer to give him. He kept asking about his brother, and the image of receiving the news of his brother's death began to form in his mind.
Amelia recalled the doctors' words that this moment would be difficult and that he might collapse when he remembered what had happened in the past. Slowly, she said:
- Daniel, your brother... he's gone. He died in the accident.
For a moment, the room was silent. Then Daniel began to shake, and tears streamed down his face uncontrollably. He cried out in pain and broke down in bitter sobs. Amelia could only hold him, sharing his grief and loss.
After a short while, Daniel calmed down slightly and asked to return to his home. Amelia recounted what Violet had done and how they were now homeless, and told him that she was living in a rented apartment and would take him there. Daniel was indifferent to what he heard or Violet's betrayal; the beautiful memories he shared with his little brother dominated his thoughts. He knew life would not return to what it was, but he realized he needed to find the strength to move forward.
When Amelia took him to the apartment she was staying in, he felt an oppressive atmosphere surrounding him. The sound of his wheelchair wheels echoed in the long corridor, and the walls of the house were covered with old photographs, mostly of him, his sister, and his little brother. His gaze stopped at a picture of his brother with a broad smile, a smile that no longer adorned his face. His body trembled, and a hot tear fell down his cheek. He couldn't hold back his tears; they flowed abundantly, and he felt the sadness engulfing him like a tidal wave. Amelia noticed his intense emotion, quickly apologized, and ran to remove the photos from the wall. She said in a trembling voice:

- I'm sorry, I didn't realize you'd be so affected. I was surprised by the hospital call and that they allowed you to leave suddenly.

But Daniel, watching her thoughtfully, asked gently:

- Don't remove them, Amelia. Leave the pictures on the walls. I feel their presence beside me, and it gives me some comfort.

Amelia stopped removing the pictures, smiling sadly as she returned to him. Daniel sat quietly, closing his eyes for a moment, sensing the memories returning through those pictures. He found solace and companionship in those faces hanging on the walls.

His sister was by his side, her eyes filled with tears. She hugged him tightly, as if trying to absorb some of his pain. She cried with him, as if tears were the only language to express her feelings. She felt his trembling warmth and his crying tore at her heart. She sat beside him on the couch, trying to comfort him. She placed her hands on his shoulder and gave him time to catch his breath.

After moments of painful silence, Daniel sighed deeply and asked in a trembling voice, as if afraid to hear the answer:

- I want to call Violet. I want to see her.

His tone carried a mix of hope and anxiety. His sister looked at him with red eyes from crying and said in a choked voice, as if struggling to find the words:

- Forget her, Daniel. She has remarried.

Her words struck him like a shattering blow, and in that moment, it felt as if his world had crumbled beneath him. He could scarcely believe what he was hearing—his face twisted in a mix of grief and betrayal. He didn't just feel lost; he felt utterly betrayed by someone he had believed truly loved him. The weight of this revelation bore down on him like a crushing force, as if everything bright and beautiful in his life had vanished.

His sister tried to comfort him, but no words could soothe the profound wound that had been inflicted. She sat beside him, gently patting his shoulder, offering the only solace she could in that dark moment—her presence. She knew that no words could ease this kind of heartache, but perhaps being close would remind him that he wasn't alone in his suffering.

Yet despite her desire to stay with him, Emilia couldn't be there constantly due to her work commitments. Recognizing this, she arranged for a companion for Daniel. A nurse was brought in to care for him at home, assisting with his daily tasks and guiding him through physical therapy sessions. She remained a constant, dedicated presence, ensuring that Daniel received the attention and care he so desperately needed during this painful chapter of his life.

One day, while performing some exercises, the nurse turned on the television to keep him occupied while he completed his exercises to avoid boredom. Suddenly, his eyes were drawn to the screen when the channel switched to a particular program. The show was broadcast on a popular channel and was hosted by a presenter named Bella.

Something about her voice captivated Daniel intensely.

Bella spoke with confidence and grace, and her voice carried a warmth and familiarity that Daniel found inexplicable, Daniel felt he knew this presenter well, but he couldn't recall how or where they had met. Memories began to seep into his mind, but they were foggy and unclear.

Daniel sat there, absorbed in trying to understand this strange feeling that had overtaken him. Bella seemed familiar, but the more he tried to remember details, the more the memories became elusive. He began to wonder: Who is this woman who seems like a part of his past? And why does he feel this mysterious attraction towards her?

After the show ended, Daniel couldn't ignore the curiosity that had ignited within him. He began searching for Bella on social media, quickly finding her profiles on Instagram and Facebook. He started following her avidly, watching everything she posted, and reading every comment and share. He wanted to know everything about her, hoping to find a clue that would lead him to the answer he was searching for. With every picture and video, he felt as if he was getting closer to uncovering the secret surrounding his relationship with this mysterious woman. For the first time in a long while, he found himself interested and eager to learn more, not only about the presenter but also about this forgotten part of his life that seemed to be awakening from its long slumber.

A few days later, Amelia was sitting next to him when she was surprised to see Bella's program airing on television. Noticing Daniel's intense interest in the program, she approached him and asked curiously, thinking he might recall something from his coma:

- Who is this presenter? You seem very interested in this show.

Daniel answered honestly:

- I feel like I know this presenter well. I feel like I know a lot about her and I feel happy when I listen to her show.

Amelia hesitated, choosing to keep silent about all she had learned during his coma. She refrained from mentioning Bella's constant visits, the quiet conversations she had shared with Daniel, or the generous donations Bella had made in his name. Nor did she reveal the opportunity Bella had provided her—a position at her father's company.

For now, she decided to let those truths remain unspoken. There would be time for explanations later. But at this moment, with Daniel finally awake, Amelia felt an instinctive need to shield him from the complexities that had unfolded during his absence. She would speak with the doctor first, ensuring that Daniel's recovery remained the priority.

Chapter Eight

One morning, while Daniel was engrossed in reading a book, he heard a soft knock at the door. Slowly, he lifted his eyes from the pages, expecting to see his sister. But when the nurse opened the door, he was stunned by the sight before him.

Bella, the presenter whose show he had been following with such interest, stood at the door with a bright smile on her face, holding a beautiful bouquet of flowers. She was dressed in an elegant lavender dress, and her eyes sparkled with vitality. A few moments passed before Daniel could grasp the situation, then he tried to get up, but was unable to, so Bella rushed over to help him.

- "Hello, Daniel," Bella said in her warm voice that he had become accustomed to hearing on screen.

She continued, saying:

- "I heard you were back home and wanted to visit you."

Daniel remained speechless for a few moments, trying to understand what was happening. He felt that words were escaping him and that all the thoughts he wanted to express were scattered in the air. All he could do was stare at her in amazement.

- "May I take a little of your time?" Bella asked politely.

- "Uh... yes, of course," Daniel stammered as he tried to sit up properly to present himself decently. Bella looked around with interest, then placed the bouquet of flowers on the table.

- "I missed you, Daniel, and talking to you. I just learned that you were out of the hospital, so I came quickly to visit you."

He looked at her, astonished, trying to absorb her words.

- "Thank you, that's very kind of you. I feel like I know you well, but I don't remember anything."
Bella smiled and said:
- "No need to thank me. We've never spoken to each other while you were fully conscious, but I used to talk to you a lot in the hospital while you were in a coma."
At that moment, Daniel began to remember something, something distant and hazy. Images and mixed feelings were slowly creeping into his mind. He recalled the warm voice that had spoken to him, and it was like the voice of the beautiful girl sitting before him. He remembered her gentle touches and the soothing encouragement he felt during his coma.
- "Did you visit me regularly?" Daniel asked hesitantly.
- "Yes," Bella replied, "I used to visit you almost every day. I felt a strong connection between us, even though you didn't know me at that time. I also visited you for my sake; I found great comfort in talking to you. I would share my problems and what troubled me, and you would listen to me in silence."
She then added with a laugh:
- "Even though listening to me wasn't exactly voluntary on your part."
Daniel felt something stirring inside him, a sense of gratitude and deep connection.
- "Thank you for everything you did for me. I can't express how grateful I am."
- "No need to thank me, Daniel. I did what I felt was necessary. I just wanted to be by your side and help you in any way I could."
As the conversation flowed smoothly between Daniel and Bella, they heard the sound of the front door opening. Amelia entered the house, and when she saw Bella sitting next to Daniel, her eyes widened in surprise.
- "Amelia!" Bella exclaimed enthusiastically as she hurried towards her to greet her.

Amelia was momentarily confused and pretended not to remember Bella well, saying:
- "Oh, sorry, I think you've mistaken me. Have we met before?"
Bella was puzzled by Amelia's strange reaction but chose to remain silent, offering a small smile.
- "No problem, you might have forgotten."
Amelia quickly left the living room, heading to her room, leaving Bella and Daniel in an awkward state. Bella returned to her conversation with Daniel, trying to ignore the tension created by Amelia's odd behavior.
- "As I was saying, I felt there was a strong connection between us, even though you didn't know me back then. I drew strength from my visits to you."
Daniel smiled, trying to get back to the conversation after what had happened.
- "I think I'm starting to understand now. Thank you for being there for me."
Daniel and Bella sat, the atmosphere filled with unspoken words. Daniel decided to open his heart and express his mixed feelings, saying:
- "Bella, from the first day I saw you on television, I felt that there was something different. I started following your show regularly, and there was something in your voice and the way you spoke that drew me to you. I wasn't just watching the show, but I was also following you on Instagram, feeling that there was a mysterious connection between us."
Bella smiled shyly and remained silent.
Daniel continued:
- "I knew I knew you somehow, but I couldn't remember anything specific. There were moments during my coma when I felt your presence, and you were talking to me."
Bella looked at Daniel seriously and said:

"Daniel, I turned to you because you have been a steadfast support throughout my ordeal. Your presence has been a silent strength, a beacon in my darkest hours. Please don't be surprised by my words. What I mean is that there are times when we feel supported by others even in their silence, while some who speak endlessly remain unaware of our true feelings. We might find that those who seem distant are closer to our hearts than those who appear near but remain beyond our understanding."

She continued:

- "During my visits, I talked to you about my life, and the things that made me sad. I wasn't sure if you could hear me, but I felt that you sensed my presence."

Bella began visiting Daniel every day at his home. She came every morning with her radiant smile, bringing fresh ingredients to prepare delicious and nutritious meals for him. She put great effort into cooking with love and care, ensuring that each meal contained the nutrients he needed to regain his strength.

Bella's visits didn't only involve preparing food. She also participated with Daniel in the physical therapy exercises prescribed by the doctors. She was by his side every step of the way, encouraging him and pushing him forward with enthusiasm and determination. They would go out together to the garden, where she would hold his hand and help him with balance, as if he were learning to walk again. Her encouragement and support gave him the strength and confidence to continue progressing.

Over time, Daniel's movements began to improve. He managed to walk without assistance and started feeling significant improvements in his health. Bella was no longer just a visitor; she became an integral part of his life. They exchanged conversations and laughter, sharing dreams and hopes with each other.

As time went on, feelings of love began to blossom between them. Daniel felt something special for Bella, a love that grew day by day. His glances became more intense, and his words grew warmer. Bella, too, felt happiness and comfort in his presence. She knew that Daniel had become more than just a patient needing care; he was the person she wanted to spend her life with.

A beautiful love story unfolded between them, born from hardships and challenges and shared destiny. Their love made every day they spent together special and filled with hope. As the days passed, they became inseparable, supporting each other in every step and living their lives with endless happiness and love.

One day, Daniel and Bella decided to go to a mall for some shopping. As they immersed themselves in their conversations, they strolled through the mall as if the world had disappeared behind the borders of that moment. Everything seemed perfect: the mild weather, the soft light dancing on the glass facades, and the gentle laughter flowing between them. Bella felt utterly at ease beside him; his presence gave her a sense of reassurance, as if he stood between her and the outside world, a world that had once been filled with pain.

As they approached a perfume store, the magic of the moment was shattered by a familiar voice that pierced her calm. It carried memories of pain and events she had long been trying to forget. She lifted her eyes to see James, the man who was once a part of her life, confidently walking toward her. In his dark suit, slicked-back hair, and a smile that combined warmth and pride, he seemed like he was trying to revive a piece of the past that had long faded.

When he finally stopped in front of them, their eyes locked for a long moment. Bella felt her heart race, but not because of James or any lingering feelings—rather, it was the weight of the memories and the pain that accompanied him. She stood firm before him, as if the past no longer had any power over her. His familiar smile no longer struck any chord within her; instead, it felt like a fleeting sensation that passed without leaving a mark.

James spoke in a tone he tried to make warm, but he couldn't hide the tension behind his voice: "Bella..."

She studied his features in silence, wondering how she had ever seen him as someone who mattered to her. After a brief moment, she responded with cold calm: "James." Her tone was like a cool breeze passing by without leaving a trace.

Daniel, who had been observing the unspoken tension between the two, gently placed his hand on Bella's waist. He didn't need words to assert his presence; that touch alone was enough to remind James that Bella no longer belonged to the past. His gaze spoke volumes, filled with confidence and love that needed no further validation.

James felt uneasy; he had expected Bella to show some kind of reaction—perhaps longing or pain—but instead, he was met with a coldness he hadn't anticipated. He tried to mask his disappointment with a false smile and then said in a strained voice, "How have you been? I haven't seen you in a while... You seem very busy."

Bella answered with firmness and a confident look: "Life goes on, James, and I'm better now than I've ever been." Her words were straightforward and strong, like a perfectly aimed arrow hitting its mark.

Daniel felt a surge of pride as he watched Bella. The woman standing beside him was no longer the girl who let James control her emotions. She was strong and fully aware of her worth.

Bella looked at Daniel with a serene smile and introduced him to James with a casual tone: "This is James... just someone from the past." She paused for a moment, then added with a smile directed at Daniel: "And this is Daniel... the man I love."

At that moment, James felt time come to a standstill. Bella's words were enough to crush any hope he had been clinging to. He tried to hold himself together, but the pain was evident in his expression.

Daniel merely offered a polite smile and greeting, but he didn't let go of Bella's hand. That touch was a clear message to James that the past was over.

With a forced tone, James said, "Well, I'll leave you two to enjoy your day..." He cast a jealous glance at Daniel before walking away.

After he left, Bella felt a great sense of freedom. Finally, she was free from the past that had long haunted her. She looked at Daniel with a warm smile and said, "Thank you for being here."

Daniel responded softly, "With you, I won't let anyone hurt you again."

James never expected that his encounter with Bella at the mall would leave such a profound impact on him. Despite his feigned smiles and hollow words, his heart boiled with jealousy and pain. He could not see the cold look she directed at him, nor the warm smile she reserved for Daniel, but he felt a shattering inside him. His pride, which had clung to the belief that he still held a part of Bella, crumbled when he realized she had moved on, leaving him behind.

Returning home, James was engulfed by a sense of desolation. That night, sleep eluded him as memories of their past haunted him relentlessly. He struggled to silence the accusing voice within that chastised him for his betrayal, but his efforts proved futile. Deep down, he knew Bella no longer harbored the same feelings for him. She no longer gazed at him with eyes filled with love and pain. Instead, she had become a confident, strong woman capable of facing the world without him.

Desperate to reclaim the lost days, James decided to visit Bella's father's house the next morning. This was not a spur-of-the-moment decision but a result of the anger and jealousy that had festered within him. He was determined to prove to himself and to Bella that he could still be a part of her life and mend the damage he had done.

Upon arriving at the house, James found Bella waiting for him at the door. She stood there with an unwavering firmness he had never seen before. No longer was she the girl who would crumble before him; she was now a resolute woman who knew exactly what she wanted and had no qualms about saying "no."

Her voice was sharp and resolute as she addressed him. "What do you want, James? Everything between us is over. There's nothing left to fix."

James stood there, bewildered, his words faltering as if they had evaporated into thin air. Finally, he managed to stammer, "Bella, I... I just want a second chance. It's not fair for you to shut me out like this. I want to explain, to make things right."

Bella's gaze was icy, her voice unwavering as she responded, "You had your chance, James, and you squandered it with your betrayal. There are no more chances. I endured so much because of you, but I've moved on. There's no place for you in my life anymore. Please, leave."

Her words were like a dagger, piercing James' chest. He had not anticipated Bella's strength or the firmness of her response. He attempted to speak again, but Bella cut him off, shutting the door in his face without hesitation.

James felt adrift, unable to grasp how everything had spiraled so dramatically. Bella, who had once been emotionally pliable, now seemed impervious to his influence.

In a final, desperate bid to regain control of the situation, James resolved to seek Emma's assistance, hoping she could persuade Bella to rethink her decision. Despite his repeated calls to Emma going unanswered, James decided to wait for her outside the company where she worked. He stood vigil at the entrance, his anxiety growing with each passing moment as he hoped for a chance to speak .

When Emma arrived at the company, James approached her with a sense of urgency and vulnerability. "Emma," he said, his voice tinged with desperation, "I realize I've made numerous mistakes, but my thoughts are consumed by Bella. I still love her deeply and can't bear the thought of losing her for good. I need to make things right."

Emma's eyes were filled with anger, her voice trembling with restrained emotion. "Where were you when Bella was suffering alone? Where were you when she was crying at night because of your betrayal? You shattered her life; she nearly lost herself because of you. And now, after she's rebuilt her strength and started anew, you come and claim you love her?"

She paused, catching her breath, before continuing with biting intensity, "You don't deserve another chance. You betrayed her, and now you want to fix things? Bella is not your plaything, and you have no place in her life anymore."

Emma rose abruptly, her voice firm and resolute. "I don't want to see you again. If you attempt to approach Bella once more, I will do everything in my power to keep you away from her."

As Emma and James faced off near the company's entrance, the tension was palpable. James, his voice rising in frustration, gestured animatedly as he tried to make his case, while Emma countered sharply, her anger unmistakable.

Unbeknownst to them, Carter was nearby, holding Bella's handbag—a bag she had inadvertently left behind, containing her office keys, credit card, and essential paperwork. When Carter saw James and Emma, he froze, his apprehension growing as he observed the heated exchange.

Emma's voice, sharp and indignant, cut through the air, "Get away from Bella! Don't even think about interfering in her life again!"

Carter watched as James walked away, his steps heavy with frustration and despair. He realized that things were escalating around him without his awareness. He turned to Emma, who stood there with her features tense and her eyes pale, as if carrying an unbearable weight.

He approached her gently and asked in a soft but cautious voice, "What's going on between you and James? You seem tense. What happened?"

Emma sighed slowly, as if trying to gather herself, then began recounting what had transpired between her and James. She told him how James had been trying hard to convince her to help him fix things with Bella, hoping the two might reconcile.

Carter listened patiently, but there was a glint of hidden cunning in his eyes. After a moment of thought, he said with a meaningful tone, "Perhaps it's best we don't tell Bella what happened. It could ruin her relationship with Daniel."

Emma paused for a moment, studying his face, then nodded slowly in agreement, as if acknowledging a hidden truth. "You're right. I won't tell her."

But she couldn't suppress her curiosity and asked, "But... what brings you here now?"

Carter smiled slightly and pulled a small bag from behind him. "You forgot this at home, and I thought you might need it."

Emma laughed lightly, as if she could finally breathe a little after all the tension she'd been through. "Thank you, Carter. I wouldn't have even noticed I left it behind."

Chapter Nine

The family gathered at house on a beautiful day, with the table filled with laughter and amusing moments. Daniel sat beside Bella, while Emma and her husband, Carter, joined along with Natalie, her mother, and Philip, her father. The atmosphere brimmed with happiness and joy, especially with Amelia and Daniel sharing funny stories from their past experiences.

Amid this cheerful environment, Carter watched Daniel with jealousy and malice. His discomfort was impossible to mask; every time Daniel spoke or laughed, it was as though a storm brewed behind Carter's eyes. Emma noticed the resentment building within her husband and tried her best to cover it up so no one else would sense his tension.

As the conversations flowed and laughter echoed through the room, Daniel suddenly stood up and addressed Philip, Bella's father, with a seriousness that commanded attention:

"Mr. Philip, I have a request I'd like to make in front of everyone today. I've thought long and hard about this, and I believe now is the right time. I truly love Bella, and I want to spend the rest of my life with her. So, I am asking for Bella's hand in marriage. Do you agree?"

A hush fell over the room as everyone awaited Philip's response. He smiled, his eyes welling up with tears of joy. He glanced at his daughter, whose eyes sparkled with happiness, before turning back to Daniel and responding:

"Daniel, you've always been a respectful and trustworthy young man. If Bella agrees, I am more than happy to bless this marriage with all my heart."

Bella's smile widened as she nodded in agreement, and joy erupted in the room. The family embraced Daniel and Bella as congratulations poured in.

While the family celebrated, Emma tried to soothe Carter, who grew increasingly agitated with each passing minute. She leaned in and whispered softly:

"Carter, this is a day of joy. Please don't let your feelings spoil it. Daniel and Bella deserve their happiness."

Carter responded with sarcasm, his tone dripping with bitterness:

"And what about my feelings, Your Highness? Whether they get married or not, it's their business and doesn't concern me."

Emma shook her head sadly and remained silent, not wanting to draw attention to their conversation. Yet her heart ached with sorrow. She wished her husband could be more kind-hearted, less consumed by his jealousy and feelings of inadequacy.

Carter forced a smile but couldn't fully conceal his anger. Deciding he needed space, he excused himself and stepped outside to calm down.

While he was gone, the family began to excitedly discuss wedding details, exchanging ideas for the celebration. Bella glowed with happiness, and Daniel's gaze never left her, as if they were living a perfect dream.

Meanwhile, Amelia sat with Natalie, and they chatted about the future. Natalie smiled warmly and said:

"I'm so happy for Bella. Daniel is a wonderful man, and I know they'll have a beautiful life together."

Amelia nodded and replied,

"Yes, I feel the same. This is just the beginning of all the good things to come."

What the family did not know, however, was that Carter's bitterness stemmed from more than just the engagement. He had long suffered under Philip's constant comparisons between him and Daniel, with Philip often accusing him of falling short. Daniel, the famous singer who had it all—success, wealth, and charm—seemed to win in every aspect of life, further fueling Carter's deep-seated jealousy."

As the celebration continued and the air buzzed with joy, Carter returned inside, his demeanor appearing calmer. He walked over to Daniel and said, his tone measured:

"Congratulations, Daniel. I wish you both a life full of happiness."

Daniel sensed an underlying tension in Carter's voice but smiled warmly, replying,

"Thank you, Carter. I hope we all find happiness."

The celebration carried on, with the family discussing future gatherings to mark the joyful occasion. Optimism filled the room, and as the day drew to a close and the house lights flickered on against the setting sun, the family began to prepare to leave. Bella embraced Daniel, leaning in to whisper in his ear:

"I'm so happy. I can't wait to start our life together."

Daniel smiled back at her, his voice filled with affection,

"Me too, Bella. This is just the beginning of our shared dream."

From that moment on, Daniel's presence in the family grew, but it wasn't just him. Amelia, too, became closer to Bella and Emma. She spent most of her time with them—whether at their parents' house, at work, while shopping, or at the club. Their bond deepened, and Amelia became an integral part of their daily lives.

One afternoon, while Amelia and Bella were out shopping, they decided to take a break at a café. Sitting together, Bella gazed at Amelia curiously before asking in a soft voice:

"Amelia, can I ask you something? Why did you pretend not to know me when I visited your home?"

Amelia stiffened slightly, her expression tightening with worry. Her voice trembled slightly as she responded,

"I didn't mean to. I was just nervous. I was afraid that your visit might harm Daniel or set back his recovery. Don't forget, Bella, your first encounter with him was in the hospital during the hardest period of his life. My biggest fear was that Daniel would somehow discover his treatment was funded by donations—and that you were the one behind it. He didn't remember anything during that time. Daniel used to watch your show regularly and followed your work. He felt like he knew you, but nothing connected in his memory. I stayed silent to protect him."

Amelia paused, glancing away before continuing cautiously, "I wanted to consult with the doctor before telling him anything. But you were already out of the country, so I felt there was no point in discussing it with the doctor. When you suddenly returned and visited our home, I panicked."

Bella frowned, surprised,

"But Daniel doesn't know anything about the donations, and he's doing well now. Isn't that reason enough to set aside all these worries?"

Amelia exhaled deeply, her eyes showing her hesitation,

"I feared that, in a moment of conversation, you might let something slip. I didn't want Daniel to feel indebted or burdened by this knowledge. I worried he might be disappointed if he learned the truth."

Bella studied Amelia, her confusion growing.

"How did you find out I was the donor?" she asked.

Amelia smiled faintly, a trace of bitterness in her expression as if she were trying to guard a secret she no longer could,

"I saw you once at the hospital. You were depositing money into his account."

Bella's confusion deepened.

"So, you knew about my visits during his coma?"

Amelia nodded, her voice softer now,

"Yes, I knew. I couldn't help but wonder—why? What was your connection to Daniel that made you so willing to help him like this? I even thought you must've known him before."

Bella looked down, her voice quieter but filled with emotion,

""I didn't know him personally; my connection to him was mediated through his songs and the screen. Yet, his voice felt incredibly intimate, as if it were channeling my own pain. Seeing him on that hospital bed, so close to the brink of death, was like being jolted awake from a nightmarish dream.

I would have given anything to bring him back, to tell him that, although he was unaware, he had always been a steadfast companion in my life. His songs had been my sanctuary, soothing the darkest corners of my soul.

I longed for something deeper than the distance of his lyrics. What began as a solitary bond through his music evolved into a deeply personal and intimate connection. I yearned for him to be more than a distant voice echoing in my life; I wanted him to be a tangible presence, a true friend. Somehow, that yearning grew into a love that felt both unexpected and fated. The depth of my feelings underscored the truth that his music was more than a lifeline—it had become a bridge to a profound and fulfilling connection I had always dreamed of."

Bella's voice trailed off, leaving the air between them thick with shared understanding.

*****

Carter was engulfed in a whirlwind of emotions that wouldn't leave him alone. A sharp pain pierced his heart as he recalled those moments when he watched Bella's family celebrate Daniel with warmth and affection—something he had always been deprived of. Jealousy was not new to him; it had been festering inside, growing deeper with every look of admiration and respect directed toward Daniel. Every time he found himself in Daniel's presence, Carter felt as though he was constantly being compared, often unfairly. Daniel was always the golden child, "the son everyone was proud of," while

Carter remained stuck in the shadows, deprived of the recognition he so desperately craved.

Carter knew that jealousy was slowly eating away at his heart, but he couldn't escape or ignore it. Every time he looked at Daniel, his own failures seemed to multiply bitterly, growing larger before him. How had Daniel managed to become the beloved, successful man while Carter could barely keep his personal life together, and even that with difficulty? This disparity drove him mad, kept him awake at night, and fueled a deep sense of injustice and helplessness that he could not shake.

He gripped his phone tightly, feeling that his only chance to rearrange things lay in destroying Daniel's relationship with Bella. If he couldn't be the man everyone admired, then he would make sure Daniel became the man who lost everything.

He called James, knowing that James shared similar motives for seeking revenge against Daniel. But Carter had a plan to manipulate James's emotions intelligently. After a few seconds, a voice came from the other end.

"Carter? What do you want?" James asked, his tone indifferent.

Carter took a deep breath, trying to control his conflicted emotions. "James, we need to talk. It's about Bella."

There was a moment of silence before James's voice came back, tense. "What do you want to say about her?"

Carter knew he had struck at the heart of the matter. "I know very well that you still care about her. And I know the real reason she refuses to return to you is because of Daniel. Bella thinks he loves her, but she has no idea he's just playing with her emotions."

James sounded doubtful. "Do you really think I'm going to believe this? That you have my best interests at heart?"

Carter smiled bitterly. "Our interests are aligned if you think about it. Why does Daniel get all the love and admiration while we lose everything? You've seen for yourself how Bella's family treats him like

the perfect person. This situation isn't just ruining your life; it's also negatively affecting my relationship with Emma and her family."
James hesitated for a moment, but he could feel the anger rising inside him. "What do you suggest?"
Carter had been waiting for this moment. "We have an opportunity now to ruin their relationship. All we have to do is play our cards right. If you can get close to Amelia, Daniel's sister, and make her fall for you, you'll be able to create a rift between Daniel and his sister. Imagine what will happen when he finds out that his sister is planning to marry you."
James pondered for a moment before asking, "And what do I gain from all of this?"
Carter let out a sarcastic laugh. "You'll get the revenge you deserve. There will be no Daniel to take everything from us anymore. He'll end up alone, and you'll watch his life crumble before you. In the end, you'll win Bella back and have her for yourself."
James could sense the plan held the kind of retribution he had long dreamed of. Carter, who had always been in the shadows, knew how to wield his dark emotions to achieve his goals.
In the days that followed, James began to execute his plan, gradually drawing closer to Amelia with charm and calculated precision. Amelia was a beautiful and intelligent young woman, and it quickly became clear that she was taken by James. It wasn't difficult for him; he had always known how to captivate women. He spoke to her kindly and paid attention to every small detail in her life, making her feel cherished and important.
As the days passed, Amelia began to fall for James bit by bit. She had no idea that he was playing a role, believing every word he said. James feigned affection, showering her with gifts and inviting her to romantic dinners. Amelia felt as if she were living in a dream.
But as James and Amelia's relationship grew stronger, tensions began to rise in Daniel's life. He felt that something was amiss, though he

couldn't quite put his finger on what it was. Preoccupied with the preparations for his wedding with Bella, there was still a looming sense of dread that something was about to go wrong.

In a decisive moment, James made his boldest move. He knew the time had come to reveal his intentions. He invited Amelia to a private dinner, and as the atmosphere became increasingly romantic, he took her hand and said, "Amelia, I've been thinking about this for a while now, and I'm certain of my feelings. I want to be with you forever. Will you marry me?"

Amelia couldn't hide her joy. She had known that this moment might come, but she hadn't expected it so soon. With tears in her eyes, she said, "Yes, James. I accept."

Amelia agreed to marry James, her heart brimming with love. She could hardly believe her life was transforming into this romantic dream. In James, she saw everything she had ever hoped for in a partner—attention, passion, and the support she craved. However, that joy began to wane as James slowly started planting seeds of doubt in her mind.

After celebrating their engagement together in a joyful and blissful atmosphere, Amelia rested her head on his shoulder. James gazed into the distance silently before breaking the calm with words that shook her to the core. He spoke with hesitation in his voice, "Amelia, there's something you need to know before we continue down this path together."

Amelia lifted her head, searching his eyes for signs of doubt or fear. She asked quietly, "What is it, James?"

He hesitated for a moment before confessing slowly, "I want to be honest with you from the start. I... I'm Bella's ex-husband."

Amelia froze in place, pulling away slightly to look at him more clearly. "What? Bella's ex-husband?!" Her voice was filled with shock and fear.

James nodded sadly and continued in a tone full of regret, "I know this must be shocking, and I didn't want to tell you because I was afraid it would affect our relationship. But you deserve the truth. I first saw you in the hospital, from afar, before I officially met you, and I was captivated by you from that moment. But Daniel... Daniel will never believe that I genuinely love you."

Amelia was utterly confused and couldn't comprehend this sudden revelation. "But why? Why do you think Daniel won't believe your love for me?"

James sighed deeply and replied with a voice tinged with sorrow, "Because Daniel will think there are ulterior motives behind my love for you. He'll believe that I'm trying to get back at him, or that I'm envious of his relationship with Bella. He won't see this as genuine love between us but as some kind of scheme."

James' words began to take root in Amelia's mind, and she started to feel anxious about how Daniel would react. She knew how fiercely protective Daniel was of his family, and he might very well reject this marriage due to the history between James and Bella. The love that was supposed to be joyful and beautiful started to become complicated and painful.

James, trying to ease her worries, took her hands tenderly and said, "But Amelia, you need to know one thing. My feelings for you are real. I love you, truly, and I want to be with you. But we have to be prepared for what Daniel might do, for what he might think of our intentions."

Amelia found herself torn inside. Should she trust James and hold on to her love for him, or should she heed the warnings in her mind and Daniel's potential concerns? There was something deep within her telling her that this love wouldn't be easy and that it might be fraught with challenges.

Despite her turmoil, Amelia chose to face her fears and continue down this path with James. She looked into his eyes and, with confidence despite the storm of emotions in her heart, said, "I trust you, James. And I'll stand by you no matter what Daniel's reaction is. If our love is real, we'll be able to overcome anything."

Yet deep down, she knew that the confrontation with Daniel would be difficult and might change everything.

In the following weeks, Amelia decided to keep her relationship with James under wraps, away from Daniel's eyes. She had a deep-seated fear that revealing their relationship could cause unnecessary tension or even jeopardize her brother's wedding. She loved James intensely, but she also respected her family's feelings and understood that a complicated relationship with someone who had a past with Bella might be a source of concern.

As time went on, Daniel began to sense something unusual. He noticed the clear changes in his sister's behavior: the long phone calls at odd hours, the persistent smile on her face, and the sudden outings she would justify with flimsy excuses. All these signs made Daniel suspect that something was happening behind the scenes.

One day, while Daniel was sitting in his home office, he decided to confront Amelia about these behaviors. He planned to speak to her candidly, to understand what was causing the sudden happiness in her life.

When Amelia walked into the office, Daniel was seated behind his desk, his eyes filled with concern. He said in a calm tone, "Amelia, can we talk for a moment?"

Amelia lifted her eyes from the papers she was browsing and nodded. "Of course, Daniel. What's the matter?"

Daniel sat on the edge of his desk, speaking with a tone full of concern. "I've noticed that you've been acting differently lately. There's a clear happiness on your face, and sometimes you suddenly leave without a clear explanation. I want to understand what's going on. Is something on your mind?"

Amelia took a deep breath, feeling a wave of anxiety. However, she decided to be honest, though she didn't mention James by name. She replied with a faint smile, "Daniel, I'm in a new relationship. There's someone in my life who brings me the happiness and attention I've been needing."

Daniel's eyes widened slightly in surprise, but he continued to listen intently. "And who is this person?"

Amelia hesitated for a moment before continuing, "I met him at just the right time. He cares deeply for me and offers me unparalleled support. I've invited him to your wedding with Bella, and I'll introduce you to him then."

Daniel smiled, feeling relieved to hear that Amelia was happy. He had no doubt that she deserved joy. He approached her and gently kissed her on the forehead, saying, "I'm happy for you, Amelia. I'm glad you've found someone who makes you happy. I hope this person is as wonderful as you say, and that you both have a bright future ahead."

Amelia felt a sense of relief from Daniel's supportive reaction. It was clear that he cared about her and wanted to see his sister happy, even if he didn't know all the details. She decided to continue keeping the specifics of her relationship with James hidden until the right time to reveal it.

As Daniel returned to his work, Amelia felt a sense of reassurance. There was hope that everything would work out smoothly, and that she could maintain the love she shared with James without any complications arising.

One day before the wedding, Bella was at Daniel's house, urging him to go for a fitting appointment with the atelier tailor to review the final arrangements for the wedding dress and suit. As they were about to leave the house, Daniel opened the door and saw Amelia descending from a car driven by James. Bella felt a twinge of unease, while Daniel's face flushed red with anger.

Daniel stormed towards James, his eyes blazing with fury, confronting him with a threatening tone, "What are you doing here? Why are you driving my sister?" It was clear that Daniel was not prepared to handle the situation calmly.

Bella and Amelia quickly moved to defuse the situation, trying to pull Daniel away from James. As James looked at Daniel with a mocking glance, he swiftly turned to his car and drove off, indifferent to what was happening behind him. This left Daniel in a state of chaos and rising anger.

Back at the house, Daniel's rage was nearly explosive. Amelia and Bella tried to calm him down, but their efforts were insufficient to ease his tense nerves. In a fit of fury, Daniel grabbed Amelia's arm tightly, causing her pain and fear. "Why were you in his car? Why are you with him?" he demanded, his voice filled with worry and anger.

Amelia hesitated for a moment, then looked at Daniel with tear-filled eyes and said in a broken voice, "James is the man I love. He's the person I told you about before."

Amelia's words hung in the air, seeming to shake Daniel's world. He yelled, "He doesn't love you! I swear it. He wants to hurt me through you, he wants to destroy my life!"

Amelia tried to defend James, trembling from the impact of Daniel's words. "James was honest with me about his past relationship with Bella, and he loves me sincerely. He doesn't want to hurt you or provoke your jealousy. We genuinely love each other."

Daniel shouted back with harshness, "He's a traitor and a liar! He'll break your heart and turn your life into a nightmare!"

Daniel's voice filled the space, making Amelia feel as though everything around her was collapsing. She tried to stay strong, but tears streamed down her face. "I love James, and I can't give him up under any circumstances. You need to understand that I can't live without this love."

In the midst of Daniel's escalating shouts, Amelia decided to leave the house. She felt that their relationship had become too strained to endure, and she resolved to seek peace elsewhere. She walked out of the house without looking back at Daniel or Bella, leaving the place with a broken heart and indescribable pain.

Amelia stumbled out of the house, her heart heavy with sorrow and tears streaming down her cheeks. The sense of betrayal and confusion overwhelmed her, driving her to run away from the house, clinging to the hope of finding a place that might ease her pain. After her departure, Bella began to confront Daniel, attempting to defend Amelia amidst the emotional storm raging through the house.

Bella stood before Daniel, her face marked by worry and sadness, her voice carrying a grave tone. "Daniel, your sister is a grown woman who fully understands She is fully aware of everything I went through with James.. Despite that, she chose to be with him. If she decides to stay with him, that is her right. You cannot control her or prevent her from making her own choices."

Daniel's eyes burned with anger, and he seemed unable to control himself. He shouted, his eyes flashing with fury, "You're right, Bella. Someone like you, used to betrayal—from your father and then from your husband—doesn't seem to care, but my sister can't endure the pain of betrayal."

Daniel's words struck Bella like a whip, causing deep pain in her heart. Each word carried the weight of wounds she had tried to avoid, and Daniel's expressed anger made Bella feel the bitterness of the negative image he held of her and her personal relationships.

Bella looked at Daniel in shock, unable to comprehend how someone could speak such hurtful words. It felt as though every word was piercing her heart, touching old wounds she had been trying to heal. Tears began to flow uncontrollably from her eyes, her face shifting between sadness and anger.

The pressure on Bella intensified from every direction, and her emotions, which she had been trying to control, began to spiral out of control. Daniel spoke with such intense fervor, as if he were exploding with rage, but his words left a profound impact on Bella, carving new wounds into her heart.

Unable to endure any more of the assault, Bella found herself overcome by a mix of warmth and conflicting feelings. She quickly stood up and took rapid steps out of the house, trying to escape the emotional turmoil that enveloped her.

Bella ran into the street, where the cold air struck her face, making everything seem to dissolve into a fog of sadness and pain. Her tears flowed freely, her steps unsteady as she struggled to maintain composure amidst the emotional collapse. Everything around her felt distant, as if she were in a parallel world where all feelings of security and stability had vanished.

******

Despite the sharp conflict between Amelia and Daniel, she couldn't ignore her deep connection with her brother. She couldn't bring herself to skip his wedding, no matter what had transpired between them. She knew that this moment represented more than just a wedding; it symbolized family, love, and the promise of a better future. She found herself moving instinctively toward her wardrobe, slipping on the dress she had chosen specifically for this day. Standing in front of the mirror, she carefully adorned herself with jewelry and applied her makeup, attempting to cover the conflicting emotions bubbling within her.

Once she was fully prepared, she went to Bella's house to assist with the final preparations. She knew that this day was important, not just for Daniel, but for everyone in her life, especially Bella, who had become more than just a friend.

On the morning of the wedding, the hairstylist and makeup artist arrived early at Bella's house to get her ready. The sun was timidly shining through the clouds, as if it was inviting joy. Everything was pulsing with life, and the atmosphere was filled with anticipation and anxiety, as it always is on special days.

Natalie, Bella's mother, was overwhelmed with excitement and joy. She entered Bella's room to wake her and start the day. But when she opened the door, Bella wasn't in her bed. The room was empty. At first, Natalie was mildly surprised but didn't panic immediately. Maybe Bella was in the bathroom, or perhaps she had woken up early and gone off to take care of something. She opened the curtains to let light flood the room and called her daughter's name softly, but there was no response.

Natalie began to feel uneasy. She searched the house, calling Bella's name with increasing urgency, but there was no trace of her. Every corner of the house held no clue as to where her daughter could be. Time passed slowly, and Natalie's concern turned into real panic. The phone calls began, but the phone rang unanswered. With each passing minute, the tension in the house grew.

As the wedding hour approached, the venue filled with guests, all eagerly awaiting the bride's entrance. Whispers spread among the crowd, and speculation quickly grew. No one knew what was happening. Where was the bride? Why was she so late?

At that critical moment, Daniel received a message on his phone. It was from Bella. With trembling hands, he opened it and read the words that completely stunned him.

"Daniel, I am deeply sorry for ruining our happiness and leaving, but your words shattered my heart, and I no longer have the strength to bear any more pain. Please, forgive me." – Bella.

Daniel felt the world spinning around him. He froze for a moment, unable to comprehend what was happening. It was as if the ground had opened beneath him and swallowed him whole, as endless questions swirled in his mind. How could Bella leave him on this day? Why? What had driven her to make such a drastic decision?

Natalie collapsed into tears when Daniel told her the contents of the message. She couldn't grasp the idea that her daughter had vanished on the day that was supposed to be the happiest of her life. The mystery surrounding the incident left everyone in shock. Questions mounted, but there were no answers.

As for Daniel, he sat down in a nearby chair, contemplating the message. His heart was heavy with sorrow and betrayal. All he could feel was deep pain and fear for a future without Bella. Despite everything, he knew deep down that the hurtful words he had said to Bella the night before were the real reason for her departure. Those words, filled with venom born of anger and old wounds, had destroyed what could have been the most beautiful day of their lives.

Despite his many attempts to reach her, Bella had made the decision to cut ties completely. Daniel, with Amelia's help, continued searching for her everywhere, but to no avail. They visited all the cafes she frequented and even the parks she would retreat to for relaxation. But Bella had vanished as if the earth had swallowed her whole.

After days of relentless searching, Daniel visited every TV station where Bella had worked. He inquired with staff and broadcasters about her whereabouts, but everyone denied seeing her. She hadn't been seen for some time, and it seemed she had abruptly left her job. Even her show, which had been a key part of her career, had been handed over to another presenter.

Each passing day deepened Daniel's sense of helplessness and despair. The words he had uttered in a moment of anger continued to haunt him. All he had left were memories and a faint hope that one day he might find her and seek her forgiveness—or perhaps forgive himself. As for Bella, she chose to distance herself from everything. She wanted to escape the pain, the betrayal she had felt, and the love that had once bound her to Daniel. She knew that leaving would be difficult, but she believed it was the only choice that could bring her the inner peace she so desperately sought.

Chapter Ten

The sadness enveloped every corner of the space, with each morning bringing a faint hope that quickly dissolved under the harsh reality. Daniel, who had once found joy in Bella's presence, was now submerged in a gloomy silence. Every corner of his home, every piece of furniture, and every picture on the walls reminded him of Bella, who had vanished suddenly like a mysterious cloud ripped from the sky, leaving behind an unfillable void.

The pain constricted his heart, as if it were bleeding from within and seeping into every part of his body, blurring the line between physical and emotional agony. His focus was consumed by the dark thoughts that roamed his mind. Every word, every action, and every moment reminded him of Bella, of her feelings that had been torn apart in his hands. Memories of their conversations, her laughter, and their promises scattered through the air, as if haunting him from every corner.

Meanwhile, Amelia carried an indescribable burden. She watched her brother, her heart bleeding from the pain, as Daniel's suffering mirrored her own. Her sense of guilt intensified daily, and she began to blame herself continuously. She believed that Daniel's harsh words towards Bella, which were merely a reaction to his fear and desire to protect her from harm—embodied by James—were the reason for Bella's departure.

Amelia could not remain idle. She felt the urgent need to find solace, particularly from James, who was supposed to be her source of comfort and support. However, since the news of Bella's disappearance from the wedding, James had completely vanished, no longer responding to her calls or contacting her since that day.

This absence stirred her curiosity and worry, and her mind clearly told her that James had achieved his goal and abandoned her as soon as Bella left Daniel. Although this truth seemed clear, her heart refused to accept it. She could not fathom the idea that James might leave her at a time when she needed him most.

Thus, she decided to seek him out, hoping he would have the words to help her through this difficult situation. She hoped that James could restore some hope and reassurance, even though her heart was overwhelmed with doubts.

On that dark day filled with conflicting emotions, Amelia went to James's house, carrying with her feelings of disappointment and anxiety. Each step toward the door felt as heavy as rocks, and every breath was filled with frustration and anger. She knocked firmly, her knocking echoing as a muffled scream of frustration and blame.

When James opened the door, his expression was cold, and his gaze aloof, as if he had not expected her. It was as though he faced her with indifference, while Amelia's heart was bursting with broken feelings.

"James, where have you been? Why didn't you answer my calls?" Amelia asked with a trembling voice, trying to mask the agony that was tearing her apart behind her strong words. Her voice quivered, but beneath the tension she tried to show lay a deep anxiety and genuine pain. Each word carried the weight of her shattered emotions, as if she were grasping at the last threads of hope in the face of harsh reality.

James gave a cold smile and invited her in. They sat in the living room, where Amelia looked at James with intense concern, while James appeared calm, as if the events he had witnessed had not affected him.

"Amelia, I think you need to know something important," James began coldly, continuing, "What Daniel said to you was true. I never really loved you. I was in your life just to stir up anger and jealousy in Daniel and Bella."

Amelia froze in place, unable to believe what she was hearing. Her tears began to flow heavily, and the pain cut through her heart. "What are you saying? How dare you do that?" she shouted with a quivering voice. "I thought we had something real, but you were just manipulating me! You were only part of your plan."

James looked at her with coldness, showing no remorse. "Wasn't it clear from the beginning? I had a specific goal, and I achieved it. You were merely a tool in my path."

James's words were like electric shocks running through Amelia's body. She felt as if everything around her was collapsing, and all her dreams were evaporating. She looked at him with eyes filled with hatred, then screamed with all her might, "You're a devil! You didn't care about my feelings; you only aimed to destroy everything!"

Amelia grabbed her bag and left James's house, heading toward her brother Daniel. She had nowhere else to go. She needed his embrace, his apology, and to hear words that would restore some hope.

When she arrived at Daniel's home, she was in a pitiable state. She entered the house and found Daniel sitting on the couch, his features etched with sadness and worry. She approached him and threw herself into his arms, crying deeply.

She whispered as she clung to him, "I'm sorry, Daniel. At first, I didn't believe you, but now I see everything clearly. You were right about James. But you were always preoccupied with Bella, and I missed you so much, my brother. Since Bella came into our lives, we haven't spent time together like we used to, and I was at my worst, searching for support. When James entered my life and showed me attention, I found myself falling for him, but now I realize I was living a big lie."

Daniel tried to find words to express his feelings. He embraced her, feeling comforted just by her return. "Amelia, don't apologize for anything. You're my little sister, and it's my duty. I'm sorry for the sense of neglect I've caused you unintentionally, but you must know that I love you very much."

Amelia looked at Daniel, tears streaming down her cheeks. "I love you, and I'm sorry for everything that happened. I thought I needed James, but now I want to be by your side. You're the person I can heal with, just like before."

Daniel's grip on his sister tightened, expressing his forgiveness and support. Yet, the days passed for him like shards of painful time. Despite his numerous attempts to fill the void left by Bella, his heart remained shattered, suffering from the anguish of her departure. Loneliness dominated him, and regret filled his moments, both day and night. He wished he could turn back time to correct mistakes and reclaim the beautiful moments that had vanished like a distant mirage.

While Daniel struggled with his heartache, Amelia stood by him, sharing his sorrow and sincerely trying to ease his suffering. She felt so much guilt that she couldn't bear the thought that she might have contributed to Bella's loss. She was determined to offer any kind of support that could help lighten the burden of grief that weighed heavily on her brother.

One day, Amelia burst into Daniel's room with a gleam of excitement in her eyes, despite the exhaustion on her face. She carried with her a new idea that could be the hope Daniel was searching for.

"Daniel," Amelia said, catching her breath from running, "I've come up with an idea that might help us find Bella!"

Daniel looked at her with renewed interest. "What's the idea?" he asked, furrowing his brow with curiosity.

Amelia took a moment to organize her thoughts before speaking with a hopeful tone. "I remembered how Bella used to always talk about your songs. She said her heart was connected to the lyrics even before she met you. What if you wrote a song just for her? A song that expresses your feelings and thoughts and dedicate it to her? It might reach her wherever she is and touch her heart."

Amelia's suggestion stirred mixed emotions in Daniel's heart. There was hesitation, but also a spark of motivation as the idea reignited his creativity. He had been struggling with a lack of inspiration, but this thought gave him hope.

"Amelia," Daniel said with enthusiasm, "that's a fantastic idea! Bella always loved my songs, and writing a special song for her could be the way to convey my feelings. I'll start right away."

Daniel quickly pulled out his phone, his fingers trembling as he searched for his manager's number. Once he heard the voice on the other end, he said with determination:

- "I want you to announce my return. No more waiting."

His manager was shocked and excited, but he could tell from Daniel's tone that there was no room for discussion. He promised to act immediately. Daniel ended the call swiftly, but he didn't stop there. As if chasing a spark from his old life, he began calling everyone he had worked with before. He contacted the composer, the lyricist, and every member of his team, saying:

- "I'm coming back. Let's start working right away."

After those calls, Daniel sat feeling disoriented and short of breath. He didn't fully understand why he was doing this. Was it because he wanted to return to the spotlight? Or was it to apologize to Bella in their own language? All he knew was that he needed to find himself again, to feel alive, and to fight once more.

As the announcement of his return drew near, his emotions became increasingly tangled. He felt joy, fear, hope, and doubt. Each night before bed, he faced himself and quietly wondered:

- "Am I doing this for myself or for Bella?"

But the decision was made, and he began preparing for his comeback with all his strength. The song gradually took shape, with its lyrics flowing from the depths of Daniel's heart. He poured out love, regret, and hope into every line. He wrote about the beautiful moments they shared, the pain of their separation, and the hope of reuniting. He tried to imagine how Bella would receive the song and how her heart would feel when she heard it.

When Daniel finished writing and composing the song, he felt a deep sense of satisfaction but also significant anxiety. He knew the song would be a cry from his heart, and whether it reached Bella or not, it expressed everything he felt. He recorded the song with great care, using a sensitive voice and instruments that reflected the depth of his emotions.

Eyes turned towards Daniel, eagerly awaiting his return. The media began to talk about him, and fans anxiously awaited his comeback. But deep down, Daniel knew that this return was more than just a professional comeback. It was an attempt to heal, to prove that he could rise again, and to win back his beloved.

Daniel released his new album after his return, achieving massive success. One of the songs from the album topped the charts, and its lyrics were directed straight at Bella. The song was a sincere expression of his feelings, capturing all the pain, love, and hope in its moving words.

When Bella heard the album, she felt another pang added to her already heavy heart. She knew that those words were meant for her, and that Daniel had not stopped loving her despite everything. Every word of the song wounded her like a sword, reminding her of the love she had lost and the pain she could not escape.

Bella was sitting in her hotel room, listening to the song over and over, tears streaming down her face without stopping. She felt the bitterness of lost love and the regret over what could have been. She wondered how she could continue living after all this pain and how she could face the coming days while carrying this burden in her heart.

******

When Violet, Daniel's ex-wife, learned of his return to the limelight, she left her new lover without hesitation. Violet was not looking for love; she sought to gain more money and influence from Daniel. She decided to return to him with all her might, relying on her acting and persuasion skills.

Despite the deep wound left in his heart, Daniel handled Violet with extreme caution. He convinced her that he believed in her false portrayal and loyalty, but he was not willing to fall into the same trap twice. He was fully aware of her hidden intentions, but chose to keep his knowledge a secret, preferring to play a game of cat and mouse with her.

Daniel began allowing Violet to visit him regularly, and in return, he also frequented her. He treated her as though he had taken her back, making her believe completely that Daniel had forgiven her and was returning to her willingly.

Daniel showed Violet fake interest, using each visit to get closer to her, but in reality, he was planning to expose her true intentions to everyone and reclaim the money she had taken from him. Violet didn't realize that Daniel was no longer the naive man she had known before; he had become more cautious.

Days went by, and Violet grew more confident that Daniel had truly returned to her. She enjoyed the moments spent with him, believing that everything was going according to her plan. But Daniel had another plan, one that relied on patience and cunning, to ultimately reveal Violet's true nature to everyone.

Amelia watched Daniel's interactions with Violet in silence and astonishment. How could he accept her back after everything she had done? How could he move past the betrayal and wounds she had caused him? These questions dominated her mind and fueled her anger day by day.

One night, while Amelia was watching from a distance as Violet frequently visited Daniel's house, she couldn't control herself. She approached Daniel after Violet had left and shouted angrily:
- "How can you accept her back after all she's done? She betrayed you and caused you the greatest pain in your life!"

Daniel smiled calmly and confidently, without losing his composure, and said:

"It's not me who gives up my right, Amelia."

When Amelia heard those words, she immediately understood what he meant. Daniel was not truly accepting Violet back; he was playing a clever game to expose her true intentions to everyone and recover the money she had stolen from him. He knew exactly what he was doing and planned every step with caution and cunning.

Amelia felt embarrassed by her angry reaction and fell silent. She realized that Daniel was not someone who could be deceived again and that he had not forgiven Violet but was waiting for the right moment to reveal her true self.

Amelia took a step back and said calmly:

- "I understand you now, Daniel."

Then she left the room without adding another word, and never brought up the subject again.

The long-awaited day had arrived. The date for Daniel's first concert after a long hiatus was announced. The audience was in a state of anticipation and expectation, as Daniel was a symbol of hope and love in many hearts. Preparations for the concert were in full swing, and the entire city seemed to be preparing for a grand event.

In the evening, crowds began to gather at the concert venue. Everyone was talking about Daniel's return and how that night would be filled with emotions and songs they had come to love. The lights sparkled, and the stage was decorated with beautiful ornaments, as if embracing Daniel after a period of absence.

The concert began amidst the applause and cheers of the audience. Daniel appeared on stage with his warm smile that had not changed, and started singing the songs that people loved. He sang with his soul and heart, as if reclaiming every moment of his past with each note he played.

Among the audience, Bella stood, trying to hide her tears. From the moment Daniel began singing the song he had dedicated to her, Bella couldn't control her emotions. She started moving slowly through the rows of the crowd, trying to reach the stage.

Daniel began singing with his warm voice:

I'm sorry... I feel ashamed

For what I said... I'm to blame

Come back to my arms... like before

My heart is happy... with you, I'm sure

I know I hurt you,

And my pain stole your sense of safety

You shared your secrets, and in my anger, I failed you

I looked like a coward, nothing but shady

You told me your story, your pain,

And begged me not to be the same

In my weakest moment... I was worse than them

The melodies of the song echoed through the hall, drifting into the souls like a gentle breeze that touched the hearts. Bella moved slowly among the crowd, her steps heavy with the longing she had waited for so long. Her eyes were fixated on one clear dream – the reunion with the lover she thought separation had taken away from her forever. She wasn't aware of her surroundings; the world seemed like a thick fog enveloping her, dissipating only before the beats of her heart that quickened with every step closer to Daniel.

And in the moment she reached the front row, she could feel his breath near her. Their eyes met, and the moment felt like it was swimming in a sea of silence; time itself paused to contemplate those glances. Daniel abruptly closed his mouth, and the words fell silent on his lips, while his eyes spoke another language, a mixture of surprise, nostalgia, and the joy that began to ignite in his weary features.

With swift but steady steps, Daniel descended from the stage. The faces around him faded like meaningless shadows, even the crowd became nothing more than a blurry backdrop. All that mattered to him was Bella, the woman who had breathed life back into his wounded heart.

He approached her until he could feel her trembling breath. Leaning in slightly, he whispered in her ear, his voice filled with longing and regret, "I'm sorry." His words were more than just an apology; they were a silent confession of all the moments of love and longing they had shared, and all the regret that had accumulated due to their separation.

He pulled her into a tight embrace, as if his arms were the only refuge that could guarantee her safety. Bella felt the warmth of his body seep into the depths of her soul, the warmth she had longed for. She couldn't hold back her tears, but she didn't need words to express her feelings. She returned his embrace with tenderness, as if trying to melt away all the pain and longing in that single moment.

Without hesitation, Daniel took Bella's hand and gently led her towards the stage. Silence filled the hall, and all eyes turned to them.

That moment was saturated with intense emotions, as the event transformed into a scene where everyone watched with anticipation, eager to see what would unfold.

Daniel embraced her once again, a long embrace as if they were trying to make up for every moment their hearts had lost. And the audience was not immune to this feeling, as their applause was deafening. But for Daniel and Bella, the outside world had faded away, leaving only the love that had reunited them.

After the event ended, Bella wandered the backstage area, her emotions swirling between joy and disbelief. As she searched for a place to catch her breath, she bumped into Violet, the woman who had caused Daniel so much pain. Bella stood frozen for a moment, unable to believe Violet was there, in the place that had witnessed her reunion with the love of her life.

Violet smiled a dry smile and said coldly, "I didn't expect to see you here, Bella."

Bella responded calmly, trying to hide her unease, "What are you doing here, Violet?"

Violet smirked slyly and replied confidently, "I'm here with Daniel. He insisted that I be by his side to witness this important moment in his return, as he told me that he draws his strength from me."

Her words were like a dagger piercing Bella's heart. She felt both anger and pain at the same time, but before she could respond, the event ended, and Daniel came backstage.

Bella glanced sharply at Violet before turning away, trying to escape the torrent of conflicting emotions that had overwhelmed her.

Daniel reached the backstage area, searching with his eyes for Bella, but Violet was the only one there. She smiled and coldly said to him, "She was here, but she left."

Daniel felt confused and hurt. He had hoped to talk to her after the event, but once again, Bella had left, leaving his heart wracked with anxiety and unanswered questions.

Meanwhile, Amelia was at home, watching clips of the event online when she stumbled upon a shot of Bella with Daniel. She paused, her heart racing, as if she had finally found proof of their reunion.

The next day, a video of Bella and Daniel embracing warmly amidst the glowing lights and crowd at the party created a huge stir on social media. The video quickly became the most talked-about topic and spread enthusiastically among people. The moments captured in the video were filled with emotion—love, joy, and hope—making it seem as though their story was far from over. What appeared to be a happy conclusion for everyone was, in fact, just the beginning of a new chapter of conflict.

Amelia, who was following the news from her room, couldn't believe her eyes when she saw the video. Her heart raced as if the blood in her veins had turned into a rapid current she couldn't stop. She pushed herself out of bed immediately and rushed to her brother Daniel's room. Bursting through the door, she ran to him and hugged him tightly, her face lit with a broad smile as she congratulated him for winning Bella back.

But instead of the joy she had expected, Daniel surprised her with a sorrowful and gloomy tone: "Bella left again."

Amelia was stunned and took a step back from her brother. Looking at him with wide-eyed disbelief, she asked, "What? She left? How? And why?"

Daniel sighed deeply before replying, "I don't know exactly... there was a conversation between Violet and Bella after the concert, and after that, Bella decided to leave. As usual, she hasn't answered my calls, and she left no way for me to reach her."

Amelia felt confused. She had hoped everything was resolved peacefully and that they had moved past this phase, but reality was proving to be different. As she tried to think of a way to reach Bella, one person came to her mind who might be able to help: Emma, Bella's sister.

With hesitation, Amelia said, "Maybe... maybe Emma knows something. Bella showed up at the concert, so perhaps she's been in touch with Emma."

Amelia decided to call Emma right away. She lifted her phone and dialed the number, and after a few rings, she was met with a sobbing, shaky voice on the other end. Emma's voice was full of anguish, barely able to speak clearly.

Amelia asked with concern, "Emma, what happened? Why are you crying?"

Emma responded between gasps of breath and tears, "I had a fight with Victor... he left the house. I don't know what to do!"

Understanding that Emma needed emotional support, Amelia saw this as her way to get closer to Bella. She gently said, "Emma, I'm coming to you. Don't worry, we'll talk, and we'll try to figure things out."

After arriving at Emma's home, Amelia sat by her side, trying to calm her down. At the same time, she was thinking of how to use this situation to reach Bella. After some thought, she suggested to Emma, "Why don't you call Bella? She's your sister, and maybe she can help you through this difficult moment."

Emma looked at Amelia hesitantly, then picked up her phone and called Bella, but, as usual, Bella didn't answer.

Quickly thinking of a plan to get Bella to respond, Amelia instructed Emma to send a message filled with desperation and worry—a message that might provoke Bella's emotions and make her call immediately. Amelia wrote the message herself: "I need you, Bella. I feel like I'm about to break down. Please, help me, I can't bear this anymore."

Indeed, it didn't take more than a few minutes before Emma's phone rang. Bella was calling, and her voice was full of concern for her sister.

Before Emma could respond, Amelia whispered in her ear, "Tell her you need to see her now, and that she must give you the address where she's staying."

Emma quickly said, "Bella, I need to see you... Can you give me the address of where you're staying?"

Without hesitation, Bella provided the address. And just like that, Amelia had gotten what she wanted.

At that moment, Amelia seized the opportunity to convince Emma that she wasn't in a state to drive and that she would take her to Bella. Emma agreed, unaware of Amelia's true intentions.

After dropping Emma off at the hotel where Bella was staying, Amelia sat in her car, basking in the feeling of triumph. She had finally gotten the address she needed. After taking Emma back home, she returned to the hotel, determined to confront Bella.

When she knocked on the door and Bella opened it, she was surprised to see Amelia standing in front of her. Bella asked in astonishment, "How did you find me?"

Amelia replied with a faint smile, "That doesn't matter now. Let me in, I need to talk to you."

Amelia entered the room and sat on a chair, her eyes filled with seriousness as she looked at Bella. "Bella, you're being unfair to Daniel. Violet's presence at the concert last night was nothing more than a trick orchestrated by Daniel to reclaim the assets Violet had stolen from him. Nothing more."

Bella listened in silence, but her face reflected a mixture of confusion and inner conflict. Amelia continued with conviction: "You need to trust Daniel more than that. He loves you and won't allow anything to stand in the way of your relationship."

Amelia paused for a moment, then said, "I just want you to think about it. Daniel is willing to do anything to win back your love, but it takes belief from your side."

After delivering those words, Amelia left the room, leaving Bella alone with her thoughts. There was an intense struggle within Bella; her emotions were torn between the doubts sown by her conversation with Violet and the love she still felt for Daniel.

Bella sat on the bed, contemplating everything that had been said. How could she learn to trust again?

Chapter Eleven

The viral video circulating on social media, showing Bella and Daniel embracing warmly amidst the party lights, was not just a fleeting trend; it ignited a fire of anger in James's heart. He sat before his screen, replaying the clip over and over, each viewing deepening the wound in his pride. His eyes burned with rage, his heart seethed with fury, and his mind boiled with thoughts of revenge.

What he found even more unbearable than the thought of losing Bella was seeing her in the arms of another man, specifically Daniel—the very man James considered a fierce and provocative rival. Each time he watched the video, he felt hope for winning Bella back slipping away, while his pride screamed inside him, accusing and tormenting him. How could she return to Daniel so quickly? How could she forget him, James, as if nothing had ever been between them?

Blinded by this anger, James decided to keep an eye on Daniel. His revenge plan began to form in his mind like a dark cloud slowly gathering. He started tracking Daniel's every move, watching his every action, like a hunter waiting for the perfect moment to strike.

During his surveillance, he noticed something that puzzled and intrigued him. He saw Violet frequently visiting Daniel's house. She came and went regularly, as if she knew the place well. Yet, Bella was nowhere to be seen. She had completely disappeared from the scene, as if she had vanished after that video.

James couldn't understand what was happening. All his expectations had pointed to Bella being with Daniel after what he saw in the video. That was the only logical explanation for things, but he was wrong.

Something was happening behind the scenes, and suspicion began to take over.

Was Violet playing a larger role than it appeared? Was Bella just a pawn in a bigger game? The questions were piling up in his mind, but one thing was certain: he wouldn't back down until he understood everything, and he wouldn't forgive Daniel for what he had done to him.

He decided to continue his surveillance, knowing that answers would come with time and that his revenge plan would eventually come to fruition. His eyes gleamed with unwavering determination as he followed Daniel from afar, resolved not to let this final chapter be written without his involvement.

******

Daniel decided to invite Violet to his home, expressing his deepest feelings. With a voice full of emotion and nostalgia, he said:
"Violet, I need to see you. There's something important I want to tell you. I can't live without you, and I want us to talk about the future. I want to marry you."
Violet felt overwhelming joy, believing that Daniel had forgiven her betrayal and that his love for her was still strong. She quickly agreed, imagining she had been given a new chance to make things right.
The next day, Violet entered the house with a wide smile, as if stepping into a world of her dreams. She found Daniel sitting in the living room, deep in thought. Daniel slowly lifted his head, looked at her with a gaze full of appreciation, and said:
"Hello, Violet. Please, have a seat."
Violet sat down, her heart pounding with excitement and nervousness. Daniel handed her a set of papers and said:
"These are the marriage documents. I want you to read them carefully and sign them."

With unreserved confidence, Violet began reading the papers, then signed them without suspecting Daniel's true intentions. She did not realize that the papers she signed were not a marriage contract but legal documents transferring all her possessions to him.

After she signed, Daniel raised his head and looked at her with a calm smile that concealed something else. He said softly but clearly:

"Thank you, Violet. Now, it's over."

Violet stared at him in shock, unable to understand what was happening. She asked with a trembling voice:

"What do you mean?"

Daniel replied with icy coldness:

"The papers you signed are not a marriage contract but documents transferring all your assets to me. I've reclaimed everything that was taken from me."

Violet was stunned and couldn't believe it. She tried to protest, but it was too late.

Violet left Daniel's home with heavy steps, her heart filled with anger and a desire for revenge. She couldn't believe what had happened and how Daniel had deceived her and taken everything she owned. It was unbearable, and she was determined to recover what she had lost, no matter the cost.

Daniel sat in the spacious living room, gazing through the large window overlooking the blooming garden. This day was the one he had been waiting for since discovering Violet's betrayal, and he had finally reclaimed everything he had lost. He seemed to be savoring the calm that followed the storm.

When Violet arrived home, her heart was pounding with a desire for revenge. She was determined to get back at Daniel, and she realized that the best way to hurt him was through his weakness: Bella.

Violet wasted no time starting her search. She began scouring social media and personal accounts for Bella, trying to connect the dots and uncover useful facts. When she found information about Bella's past relationship with James, she felt a sense of satisfaction. This information was like a ticking bomb ready to explode, and she had a clear plan to use it for her revenge.

Violet quickly decided to go straight to James's house. Her nerves were on edge, and every step toward his home was filled with the tension of vengeance. She knocked on the door forcefully, her heart racing. When James opened the door, confusion was evident on his face. He hadn't expected Violet's visit, and it was clear that her sudden appearance had a significant impact.

James looked at Violet in surprise as she asked with curiosity:

"I know you well. You're Daniel's ex-wife, aren't you?"

Violet replied with a tone full of pain and anger:

"Yes, I'm Violet, Daniel's ex-wife. He left me for Bella."

James was somewhat shocked. He was surprised that Violet had come to his home, but he hadn't yet realized the full extent of her visit's impact. Violet began recounting her story, trying to convince James that Bella and Daniel had betrayed them both, and that their relationship had started even before their separation.

With confidence, Violet started to claim that Bella had been involved with Daniel for a long time and that there was clear betrayal on Bella's part. Her words were carefully chosen, leaving no room for doubt and intensifying James's suspicions.

James sat before her, his expression gradually shifting from confusion to deep resentment. He didn't need further provocation; his feelings toward Daniel were already filled with jealousy and bitterness. What heightened these feelings further was Violet's confirmation of those old emotions.

Once Violet had stirred James's anger, he wasted no time using these burning emotions for revenge. His heart was ablaze with the fire of vengeance, and his thoughts surged like a raging torrent, filled with pain and anger. He decided to call Bella, and every part of him felt the urgency and desire to settle scores.

James grabbed his phone, his hands trembling with tension. He felt his heartbeat accelerating as if a storm was churning inside him, while his fingers dialed the numbers quickly, as if racing against time to unleash a new storm. He pressed the call button, took a deep breath, trying to control the anger that was consuming him.

When Bella answered the phone, her voice was faint and hesitant, completely unaware of what was coming. But James's voice carried the weight of his emotions, devoid of any dispute.

"Bella," James said with a voice filled with a mix of anger and bitterness, "you think you've escaped punishment, but now I know everything. I know you were involved with Daniel even before we separated."

James's words were like a lightning bolt striking Bella's heart. She had never expected James to call her in this manner, and with every word he directed at her, Bella felt her heart breaking with pain and fear. James's voice was laced with bitterness, and the vengeful words he spoke were like fire igniting every hope in her heart.

"You betrayed me," James continued, his voice growing more intense, "and now I will take revenge on you and Daniel by any means possible. I will make your lives hell, and I will burn your heart as you burned mine."

James spoke as if he relished fueling Bella's pain. His words were like drawn swords, inflicting new wounds on her heart. Bella felt something exploding inside her, as if she was being dragged into the depths of hell. Fear and sorrow surged within her, making her feel like she was sinking into a whirlpool of frustration and despair.

"I will make you both feel every pain I suffered," James added, "you won't just regret it, but you will feel the impact of your actions on every moment of your lives."

James ended the call with a sharp motion, leaving Bella in a state of complete shock. The words he had spoken still echoed in her mind like a frightening echo. Bella felt as if she was drowning in a sea of tears and pain, with no escape from the nightmare that James had imposed on her.

Calmly, James followed Daniel's car through the dark city streets. He knew the route Daniel would take and seized every opportunity to position himself for his plan. Eventually, he waited until Daniel reached a secluded area of the city with little traffic.

At a critical moment, James accelerated his car toward Daniel's vehicle and violently collided with its side, causing Daniel's car to overturn several times before coming to rest on the roadside. The crash was so horrific that everything turned into utter chaos.

Inside the wrecked car, Daniel was surrounded by shards of glass, his body torn apart by pain from every direction. He felt excruciating pain in his chest and legs, and he began to lose consciousness gradually. Blood was flowing from his wounds, and each breath was accompanied by intense agony.

James took advantage of the chaos caused by the accident and quickly left the scene, leaving Daniel in critical condition. He knew the injuries he inflicted wouldn't be superficial, and the pain would be enough to make Daniel remember this incident for the rest of his life.

Daniel was taken to the hospital, where the pain from his injuries intensified. This moment was pivotal because it was the same hospital where he had met Bella in the past. The calm surrounding the hospital contrasted sharply with Daniel's previous chaos. He slowly opened his eyes, catching glimpses of the bright lights in the emergency room, but he couldn't distinguish the faces around him.

Doctors worked swiftly to stop the bleeding and treat the severe injuries. Daniel was in excruciating pain, and his faint voice expressed the suffering he felt. Surgeons attempted to stabilize his broken bones and tend to his wounds, but the situation was extremely critical.

Meanwhile, James watched from a distance, confident that his plan had succeeded. He felt a sense of triumph seeing Daniel in such a dire state. Revenge had turned into a feeling of total control over another person's life, and he was planning to inflict more pain and suffering on Daniel.

Bella sat quietly in her room, scrolling through social media when urgent news started pouring in. The headline that caught her attention was "Terrible Accident Involving Daniel." Her heart stopped for a moment as she quickly read the details. Daniel had been in a serious accident and was taken to the hospital in critical condition.

Without hesitation, she rushed to the hospital, her heart racing. She tried to keep negative thoughts at bay, but fear overwhelmed her completely. When she arrived at the hospital, she was in a state of deep sorrow. She rushed to the emergency department, her eyes searching for any sign of Daniel. At that moment, she saw a group of nurses wheeling a stretcher down the corridors. She immediately recognized that it was Daniel.

She shouted his name as she ran after the moving stretcher:

"Daniel! Daniel!" Her voice was filled with pain and fear.

The nurses tried to stop her, but she was determined to reach him.

"Sorry, ma'am, you can't go in. He needs to stay in intensive care."

Bella stood behind the glass, her eyes overflowing with tears as she watched Daniel. She saw the doctors working hard to save him, surrounded by machines monitoring his condition. With a trembling voice, she began calling his name, trying to reach him through the veil of pain and suffering:

"Daniel... Daniel, I'm here. Please, be okay."

Slowly, Daniel began to open his eyes, as if her voice had finally reached his heart. His vision was blurry, but he could see her standing there. He waved his hand slightly to reassure her that he was alright.

At that moment, all their feelings of love, fear, and hope were encapsulated in a single glance.

Bella started crying intensely but felt relieved that Daniel was still alive.

"I'm here, Daniel. I will never leave you."

That gesture marked a new beginning for them. Daniel gradually regained consciousness and continued to recover slowly. Bella was by his side every step of the way, providing him with the love and care he needed.

At that moment, Daniel understood how much Bella meant to him. "I now realize that I can't live without you, Bella. You have always been the most important part of my life," he said.

Bella smiled through her tears and replied, "And I too, Daniel. I will never leave you again."

The next morning, Bella sat in the hospital waiting room, trying to calm herself after a long night of worry and tears. She reflected on everything that had happened and the moment she realized that Daniel's accident was James 's fault.

When a nurse approached her to inform her that the police had arrived and wanted to speak with her, she felt a lump in her throat. She knew this moment was crucial and that she needed to be strong enough to give her testimony.

Bella entered the temporary investigation room at the hospital, where a police officer was waiting for her. She sat calmly and took a deep breath before beginning to recount the events.

"I am Bella, James 's ex-wife. A few days ago, James threatened me, saying he would take revenge on Daniel . I thought it was just a threat to scare me, and I never imagined he would carry out such a heinous act."

She paused, struggling to hold back her tears, and continued, her voice trembling, "James was always violent and unpredictable. After we broke up, he wouldn't stop trying to make up. When I refused, he threatened me and accused me of cheating on him with Danielle before we broke up."

Her tears fell freely, and she broke down sobbing, "I wish I had set aside my pride and told Daniel. Maybe I could have saved him from this pain."

The officer carefully wrote down her statement and said gently, "Your testimony is very important, and we will take all necessary steps to ensure a fair trial."

In the following days, James was arrested and investigated. The evidence and testimonies collected by the police were strong enough to press charges against him. Amelia was detained in jail, awaiting trial.

During the trial sessions, Bella appeared as a key witness and recounted her story before the judge. She was strong and determined to see justice served. Ultimately, Jameswas sentenced to a long prison term as punishment for his crimes.

When Bella left the courtroom, she felt a heavy burden lift from her shoulders. She knew Daniel would need time to recover, but she was grateful that justice had been served

Months passed, and gradually Daniel fully regained his health. He left the hospital with a bright face, with Bella by his side, who had never left him for a moment during his recovery. Their love was stronger than ever, and they decided it was time to complete the wedding they had always dreamed of.

The preparations for the wedding became the talk of social media. Every detail was meticulously arranged, aiming to make the event spectacular, reflecting the strength of their love and their resilience through difficulties.

On the awaited day, the venue was adorned with white flowers and shimmering candles. The atmosphere was filled with magic and romance. Guests spoke of the venue's beauty and the meticulous arrangements, eagerly anticipating the sight of the bride and groom. Bella appeared in her dazzling white gown, sparkling like a princess. Her father took her hand, filled with pride and joy.

As Bella reached the wedding platform, her father approached Daniel and spoke with sincerity: "Daniel and bella , I am proud of you both and wish you a life full of happiness and love."

He then personally handed Bella's hand to Daniel. Daniel and Bella exchanged looks filled with love and gratitude. This apology was a significant moment, rekindling the meaning of forgiveness and reconciliation.

The ceremony began, with lights twinkling around them. Romantic music filled the air, and friends and family surrounded them with joyous enthusiasm. It was an unforgettable night, full of happy moments and warm feelings.

Pictures of the wedding spread quickly on social media, becoming the talk of the town. Everyone praised the beauty of the event and the strong bond between Daniel and Bella. The images of happy moments and smiles told a story of true love that overcame all challenges.

At the end of the celebration, as the lights dimmed and the couple was alone, Daniel looked at Bella and said, "This is a new beginning for us. We have overcome all obstacles and become stronger. I'm lucky to have you by my side."

Bella smiled and replied, "And I too, Daniel. This is our day, and we will never forget it. It was different, but it was beautiful with you."

The joyful celebration ended, and the lights began to fade gradually as the stars twinkled in the sky, blessing the newlyweds. Daniel and Bella decided it was time to head to their new home, beginning a new life full of hope and love.

The newlyweds drove off in their car decorated with flowers and white ribbons, amidst the applause of friends and family. The atmosphere was filled with happiness and joy, with smiles on everyone's faces.

Before they got into the car, Amelia, Daniel's sister, hugged him warmly and said, "Congratulations, dear brother. I wish you both a life filled with love and happiness."

She then turned to Bella, smiling warmly. She embraced Bella in return and whispered in her ear, "Thank you, Bella. For making my brother happy."

Bella felt love and appreciation filling her heart. She embraced Amelia warmly and said, "I love you, my little sister. We are family now."

The newlyweds drove off in their car decorated with flowers and white ribbons, amidst the applause of friends and family. The atmosphere was filled with happiness and joy, with smiles on everyone's faces.

Before they got into the car, Amelia, Daniel's sister, hugged him warmly and said, "Congratulations, dear brother. I wish you both a life filled with love and happiness."

She then approached Bella, smiling warmly. In response, Bella embraced her and whispered in her ear: "Thank you, Bella, for bringing happiness to my brother."

Bella felt love and appreciation filling her heart. She embraced Amelia warmly and said, "I love you, my little sister. We are family now."

The newlyweds got into the car and drove towards their new home, leaving behind the memories of the grand celebration and the happy moments that brought together family and friends.

Bella sat next to Daniel, feeling content and happy. She looked at him with a bright smile and said, "I love you so much, Daniel."

Daniel gently held her hand and replied, "I love you, Bella. This is our special day, and we will never forget it. I'm grateful for every moment we spend together."

Bella smiled and responded, "And I too, Daniel. Let's start our new life and build new memories filled with love and happiness."

That moment marked the beginning of a new journey, full of hope and shared dreams. The newlyweds set out towards a future filled with possibilities, knowing that their love would always be their source of strength and happiness.

*****

Almost a year had passed since Daniel and Bella's wedding, and their love continued to grow stronger with each passing day. During this time, Bella learned to move past the pain of the past and forgive her father for his wrongs against her mother, thanks to Daniel's constant support.

On a bright day, they were blessed with their first child. When Bella held her baby boy for the first time, she felt a wave of joy and love wash over her heart. They decided to name him after her father, in appreciation of the efforts he made to improve his relationship with Bella and her mother.

Bella's mother stood beside the bed, her face filled with a smile of contentment. She approached her husband and took his hand, in a moment of reconciliation and renewed love between them.

Bella spoke with deep emotion, "I am happy that we have reached this stage. Thank you, Daniel, for your support and love. By God's grace and with all of you, we are now a strong family."

Daniel smiled and replied, "We will always be here for each other, and this is the new beginning of our life as a family."

Bella embraced her son, feeling that the love and happiness surrounding them now were the results of patience, strength, and faith.

As time passed, Daniel and Bella became symbols of harmony and understanding within their family. Daniel was not only a loving husband to Bella but also became a close friend to vector, who had initially harbored resentment and jealousy towards him.

Daniel began to approach vector in a natural and straightforward manner. He invited him out for coffee, shared in some sports activities he enjoyed, and they talked about life and the challenges they faced. Gradually, feelings of resentment faded, replaced by friendship and trust.

One day, while Daniel and vector were sitting in a beautiful garden, vector joked, "I don't know why I didn't like you in the past," and laughed heartily.

Daniel smiled and said, "The important thing is that we are friends now. You're like a brother to me, vector ."

Daniel's efforts extended beyond vector . He worked hard to improve his relationship with Philip as well. He started visiting Ali regularly, discussing life and shared interests. He also invited Bella's father to spend time with the family, both at family gatherings and special occasions.

Over time, the relationship between Daniel ,Philip and vector grew strong, characterized by respect and understanding, which contributed to building a solid family bond.

As for Emma and vector , the positive changes in the family significantly impacted their relationship. Emma felt comfort and security, leading her to reconsider her relationship with vector. Gradually, they grew closer again and decided to give their love a second chance.

One day, Emma sat beside vector and said with heartfelt emotion, "I think we can start anew. Things have changed so much, and I feel we deserve a second chance."

vector smiled and replied, "Yes, Emma. I truly wronged you in the past. I love you deeply and hope you will forgive me."

A few months later, they received joyful news: Emma was pregnant with their first child. The moment was filled with joy and happiness, and they couldn't wait to share the news with their family.

Everyone gathered at Bella and Daniel's home to celebrate this happy news. The atmosphere was filled with love and optimism, with everyone feeling that they were a united family.

In this way, God's compensation for Daniel and Bella was great, bringing together two souls that had been searching for love and happiness.

About the Author

MK Maximous, a former biotechnology researcher, has transformed into a novelist, seamlessly blending science and fiction in her storytelling. During her university studies, she pioneered research into novel cancer treatments using bee venom, significantly influencing her writing. This rich scientific background imbues her stories with unique intellectual depth, as she intertwines scientific knowledge with boundless imagination.

www.ingramcontent.com/pod-product-compliance
Lightning Source LLC
Chambersburg PA
CBHW071441130726

47997CB00006B/2181